THE
WRONG
MAN

MATTHEW LOUIS

THE WRONG MAN

VIGILANTE
CRIME & PULP

VIGILANTECRIME.COM

The Wrong Man by Matthew Louis

Published by Out of the Gutter and Gutter Books, republished by Vigilante Crime, an imprint of Gutter Books.

THE
WRONG
MAN

ONE

Maybe you've been to a party like this. The yard is dirt, the dog is locked away somewhere so he won't go nuts but his house, built on a pallet, is there under the little oak tree by the fence, along with his water bucket and food bowl. The place was hard to find, on a long road that threads the hills between towns, and this is why a speed metal band can set up on the back deck. The band members have pushed the old Weber barbecue and the yard furniture aside and stacked up their hard-bought amplifiers and PA speakers, put the shining drum set in the back by the kitchen window, the microphones up front by the neglected flower beds.

You watch them taking the stage for their second set, ducking under guitar straps, saying "check" into the mics. They are ethnically diverse—well, white and Mexican—and look like heroin junkies. The vocalist, a skinny, vaguely pretty young man with shaggy black hair and a shoulder tattoo, scans the dozens of people assembled in the dirt, drinking Miller from red plastic cups. He comes out with a sentence or two of self-conscious banter before he gives the four-count and the band, called Slow Death, unleashes a prolonged, hammering explosion of noise and screaming that reverberates up to the clouds where it breaks up and dissipates over the countryside.

It's ten-thirty at night but you squint against the glare. Four or five floodlights are positioned around the yard, gleaming off people and objects, sending stretched, black shadows off in peculiar directions. A few of the drunker, more precocious attendees start a mosh pit, churning up a fog of dust that obscures your view of the band and causes everyone else to draw back and swipe their hands through the air. There are Mexicans, there are whites. There are longhairs, there are Mohawks, there are crew cuts. Some of the people have passed the point in their lives when it's acceptable to be at a party like this—pushed onward into their late thirties, even—but they're still waiting for adulthood to strike, for real life to kick in, and until that magic happens they're staying high and spending their Saturday nights as they did when they were sixteen.

If you haven't been to a party like this you may not understand why I was so desperate to leave. I was closing in on thirty now and was, for my part, trying to assume the role of Adult. I had a pregnant fiancée at home and a daily routine that I took comfort in. I had, I felt, left behind this world of wasted, loud, arrogant small-town heroes. I was attending Morse Junior College during the day, getting homework done while I cashiered at Vanguard Liquors in the evening and then driving back to my apartment and sleeping peacefully with Jill. I was going to get a degree in business administration, own a gas station or a Subway franchise, for fuck's sake, and here I was at the hour when I would normally be flossing my teeth, watching over-the-hill teenagers stomp around in the dirt to an incomprehensible cacophony of shit.

I narrowed my eyes at Rich Channing, coming toward me through the clouds of dust. He was supposed to check in with his friend, the drummer, so I could go, but I had watched Rich wander inside the house instead. He strode up now, positioned himself shoulder-to-shoulder with me and leaned over, his beery breath drifting past my nose. "I can't talk to him until his set's over. Anyway, I don't think it's gonna work out. Can you gimme a ride out of here?"

I turned to him, made a face and said, "Dude, what the fuck are you talking about?" He had shown up as I was closing the liquor store and begged me for a ride. He said he'd get me some money for gas, said the band was badass and I'd like them, said the drummer was his bro and was putting him up and he wouldn't have anywhere to sleep tonight if he didn't get to this party.

It was the last reason that made me sigh and say all

right. Rich had looked like death under the fluorescents, his skin pale and waxy, blackened hammocks drooping under his eyes. He had been flying high for a few days, I could tell, and now the drug engine had sputtered and died and he was in freefall, beginning his screaming descent back to earth. I figured I had to take him somewhere—it was that or deal with him begging to sleep at my place.

Rich was one of those people you try to help against all your better judgment, one of those people you're bound to from the past, who flaunt their blundering stupidity before you with such blank-faced sincerity that you think you can just explain the obvious to them and they'll stop destroying themselves. We had a history of close friendship that spanned back to when we were both eleven and I had never quite been able to give up on him. Looking back, it was a form of insanity in me.

Now, at this absurd party, he laid his gaze on me hard, trying to communicate with a look so he didn't have to yell over the band. The glare of the floodlights had a dramatic effect, casting deep shadows off his prominent, straight nose, blackening the dips under his cheekbones. At twenty-nine Rich was a good-looking guy, dark-haired, long-legged and well-proportioned. He brought his face close to mine and said, "Sam. Listen, dude, let's get the fuck out of here. I'm serious."

I thought a moment, shrugged and said, "Sure, whatever." We started out of the yard, saying goodbye to a few people on the way, then went around the house and back to where the cars were racked up on the shoulders of the long driveway.

As we rolled down onto the public road Rich could contain himself no longer and said, "Check it out, dude!" and lifted the tinfoil out of the crumpled paper bag he had under his jacket and opened it so the damp reek of pot filled the car. The foil package was the size of a brick.

"Where the fuck did you get that?"

"In the back room of that house, by the pisser, dude! I could smell it from down the hall. It was right there waiting for me on the bed!"

"You telling me you stole it?"

"Fuck that. There's fucking two hundred people there. The dumb fucks left the weed just sitting there. How they ever gonna know it was me?"

I opened and closed my hands on the steering wheel. A bad feeling, something like a premonition, was creeping up my back, hardening my shoulder muscles. "There were maybe eighty people there," I said. "And we're the only ones who just showed up and left. This is dumb, man. This is no good. What do you think you're gonna do, sell it?"

"Not all of it!"

"So think about it. You're all of a sudden gonna be selling weed around town at the same time these people's weed's gone up missing, you fucking moron?"

He was quiet. We were gliding down a black stretch of road bordered by thick clumps of trees on one side and tall hills on the other. I watched the headlights scudding over the asphalt ahead of us and tried to control my blood pressure with steady, deep breaths.

"I'll figure something out," he said, and I glanced over and could make out his frown.

I blew out a slow breath. "Listen, what you ought to do is get rid of it and deny everything. How much money you think that represents, Rich? People are deadly serious about this shit."

"How about this, Sam? We can go to San Jose—"

"Fuck no. I've got nothing to do with this, you hear me? Don't even try to drag me into it."

He lowered his head and sniffed. "This is what? A thousand bucks? I'll cut you in, man, fifty-fifty—"

"I don't even want to talk about it, all right?"

I slowed and hit the turn indicator, put it into second while still rolling, let the clutch out and accelerated left onto San Gabriel Road.

"I'm just trying to think," Rich said.

I broke out laughing. "Little fucking late for that!" Then I narrowed my eyes at a car passing us and breathed, "*Oh shit.*"

Your mind puts those pieces together fast and you see the cop car before you comprehend it, even on a long dark road late at night. It was coming toward us and my headlights shaped the light bar on top, the glossy black hood and the car-pusher in front of the grill, and the slow horror of it rolled down onto my thoughts like a mudslide. I glared into my rearview, and when I saw the cop's brake lights ignite, my blood got prickly cold.

"We're getting pulled over, man," I said. "You roll down the window and get that fucking reek out of here and you chuck that fucking weed right now—"

"No way, man!"

"Rich, I'm serious. I'll fucking kill you."

"No way."

"Rich, that much weed is a felony! Think about it. If I get arrested for this shit, I'm gonna rat your ass out, tell everyone what happened, I swear to God. Chuck it, man! You can come back for it later!"

I could sense a light flick on in his brain and he said, "All right! All right!" His fingers flew, sealing the pot back in the foil and rolling the foil back in the paper bag. The window cranked down, filling the car with a whoosh of cool air. His hand reared back and he tossed it out toward the drainage ditch that parallels the road for six miles or so. I watched in my mirror as the cop completed his U-turn and fell in a quarter mile behind me.

Nothing came of it. I wound up with a fix-it ticket for a taillight that wasn't out but was so dim it didn't count. The cop was improvising. He was disappointed by the prospects I presented, as I was clearly sober and denied having so much as a sip of beer. I didn't even get asked to step out of the vehicle. We didn't have seatbelts on, but my car was a '64 Fairlane and I guess we were exempted somehow. The cop didn't bring it up anyway.

As the police cruiser slid past us and I started my car again, Rich said, "Let's go back and get it, dude!"

"Sure, guy." I made the OK sign with my right hand.

"We're gonna go hunt for a pound of pot in a roadside ditch at eleven at night when we know cops are prowling around."

"Yeah, you're right. That's cool. I'll come back for it tomorrow. Don't worry about it."

"I'm not."

"Hey, Sam?" I was shifting into third and I could feel his stare bearing hard against the side of my face. "Can I crash on your couch? Just for tonight?"

"Fuck."

"Just sleep, man. I'll get up and leave early. You won't even know I'm there. Come on. I'll tell you the truth, bro, I haven't slept in a couple days. I'm starting to come apart."

I let out a long breath. "My chick, Rich...you know, she's not gonna like it. She's already pissed at me for not coming home after work." I threw him a look. "You better be dead silent and then leave when the sun comes up."

"I will, man. I swear to god. And watch, I'm gonna get that weed and make some money, and I'll cut you in, real quiet-like. Nobody'll know."

"Please don't," I said.

I opened the door and stopped, turned and put my hand on Rich's chest before he could trail in after me. "Just a minute, man."

Jill's eyes flashed anger when she realized I wasn't alone. She had been watching a talk show, waiting up for me, and she was in her sleeping outfit of panties and a filmy tank top. Now she huffed a little and stood, snatching up the blanket we kept on the couch and covering herself, then grabbing the remote and killing the TV with a vicious little thumb-punch.

I let Rich in. "You guys ever met? Jill, Rich. Rich, Jill. Come on," I said to Jill, "let's go to bed, all right? I told Rich he could crash on the couch."

I closed the door and there was an awkward moment while Rich muttered greetings and Jill tried to stifle her irritation. Then Jill said, "Well, goodnight," and hustled past, and I was suddenly seeing her through Rich's eyes, seeing how far-off and amazing she must look to him with her breasts rounding out the front of the blanket, her long, delicate neck under the wedges of her blonde pageboy cut, her flushed cheeks and wide red mouth.

All Rich said was, "Damn, your chick is cute, Sam."

"Rich, just don't ever think about her, okay?" I said, surprising myself with my tone.

"Nothing like that, bro! Relax!" He held up his hands in a *whoa!* gesture, then changed the subject. "Hey, you got a sleeping bag or something?"

I found my old sleeping bag in the hall closet, tossed it to him, and went to brush and floss.

Five minutes later, in bed with this warm incredible girl while that poor idiot stole a few hours of peace and safety on our couch, I tried to explain it to Jill, speaking just above a whisper. When I was eleven, my parents were killed and I came to this town to live with my grandparents—this part she knew, of course, but my point was that, by luck, a kid who happened to be my age, Rich, had lived two houses down. "We were like brothers," I said, halting, hearing how corny it sounded. "I mean, you know, we did everything together, night and day."

"You mean you were *best friends*?" Her eyes were wide and mocking.

I knew she was in a mood about me not only coming home late, but showing up with this strung-out fool, and I said, "Yeah, I guess that's it." I reached over and snapped off the bedside lamp, then lay on my back, staring at the ceiling with my hand resting on the lush hill of her hip.

"Goodnight, Jill."

"Goodnight."

I exhaled the last of my energy and closed my eyes, feeling the city of Blackmer stirring in its restless sleep outside, feeling my thoughts starting to succumb to the strange logic of dreams. *Like brothers*, I thought. What a joke. Like a couple of broken pieces of a complete human being. I was smarter, more emotionally balanced, certainly a better athlete, but Rich had the attitude. Rich was attractive to girls, knew how to talk, was an incurable smart ass, was *cool*. Right up into high school, whenever he cut or stayed home sick I wound up sitting there and watching the other kids. Eating lunch alone, slinking off and hiding out in the library.

It's been a problem my whole life, this goddamned timid streak. For most of my youth I had Rich to shove me or drag me into the mix, to get me into fights and, later, to make up for it by getting me laid. I used to need him, to lean on him, to seek his approval. But now I thought of the person out there on the couch and I felt nothing except a low-frequency disgust. Who gave a shit anyway? Nobody wanted to hear about Rich's depressing life, nobody wanted to understand, so there was no point to any of it. The guy was broken. Too many years with nobody caring. Too many fucking drugs. Half the circuits on the board had been cooked.

When I awoke in the morning around seven, the sleeping bag was rolled up and tied off, sitting on the end of the couch, and Rich was gone, out wandering the early morning streets doing god-knew-what—panhandling next to the McDonald's or maybe already trying to get a line on another fix.

I never found out if he went back for the weed. Probably some fieldworker or bottle-picker found it Monday morning, and that was the end of Rich's career selling pot.

The way things happened, it didn't matter.

TWO

I didn't hear about it until I went back to work at Vanguard Liquors Monday afternoon. The guy who worked from seven a.m. until two in the afternoon, when I came on, sold pot himself, right from behind the counter, and he had an amiable relationship with most of the lowlifes on this side of town.

He was called Sully although his last name wasn't Sullivan, but Sulazar. I liked him well enough and he seemed to like me—at least we had never had other than respectful words. He was a shrewd guy. His face was a Halloween mask, a wasteland of pimples and pitted scars, but he got by and got ahead and was in a leadership position in a crowd of guys who all thought they were world-class thugs. He had learned the virtue of taciturnity. Unless he had something to say he tended to just listen to you and respond in clipped, monotone phrases, single syllables, or grunts.

Today he watched me as I entered the store, kept his eyes on me until I was behind the counter with him, and said, "You heard about your buddy, Rich?"

"No."

"He got killed—almost. You better watch your back."

"*Me?*" I felt my eyes go wide.

"I'm just telling you what I heard. They say you guys stole some *shit*." He put special emphasis on the word *shit*, as if he found this street jargon amusing. He had a way of speaking that made it seem he was always leading up to a punch line.

I started to say *no*, but he said, "Know that dude, Owen Ferguson?"

I said, "Yeah."

"He fucked your buddy up is what I heard. Black-jacked him. Rich is in the hospital 'n' shit."

"This has got nothing to *do* with me!"

"I'm just telling you what I heard," Sully repeated. "You guys gotta give 'em money or something. I don't know. Owen *lives* over there," he pointed to Rancho Bonita, the Mexican restaurant across the parking lot, "and he's probably gonna come over and see you tonight. You might want to be ready. That's all I'm saying."

I was trying to grasp it, my eyes losing focus as I stared at the diamond and gem-colored bottles of hard liquor in their neat shining rows on the far wall, watching them through the dust specks swimming in a ray of afternoon sunlight. "Hey," I said, looking back at Sully. "Thanks for taking the trouble to warn me, man. I appreciate it."

He looked at me for a moment, thinking, and when he spoke, his casual mockery of everything in the world wasn't present for once. "Just be aware, dude," he said. "These are the gangsters you don't fuck with around here. What I heard is, Owen was trying to kill your buddy, and it didn't work out, but Rich has got it coming sooner or later. And you're next on the list. All kinds of people saw you guys at that party, saw you leaving, and *you* got named. I'm just warning you, dude. You're in it."

I nodded again. "Okay. Thanks, man. Seriously." It seemed I couldn't quite fill my lungs. You live like a maniac through your twenties, do so many idiotic things for so long, and nothing much ever happens. And here, now, I didn't want to take any chances in my life, just wanted to get the fuck home and work my job and go to my classes, and the worst kind of trouble had latched itself onto me. It was like winning some lottery of shit luck.

Sully had his jacket draped over his arm now and was fitting the earbuds of his iPod into the sides of his head. We didn't close out the register between shifts and he simply stepped away from it as the door buzzer sounded and a customer came in. I had to step up to my post behind the register and as I did Sully said, "Adios, Sam," and sauntered out.

By the time I closed the cash drawer and thanked the customer, Sully's VW was gliding away through the parking lot. I was alone, wondering what the fuck I was supposed to do now.

I wouldn't claim to understand gang politics in this town any more than a man outside a zoo cage can understand how hyenas choose their alliances and organize their hierarchy. All I know is the Mexicans who shoot and beat on each other and operate Blackmer's drug trade aren't anything like the East Coast gangsters you see on TV. The organized criminals in this town will never run bookkeeping operations or protection rackets or have the mayor or chief of police on their payroll. They have only one consistent trait that I've ever observed: massive, steel balls. Their only rule of conduct is *Don't go out like a pussy*. They don't give a second thought to trading blows on the sidewalk downtown with complete strangers who wear the wrong color or say the wrong word in passing. They keep pit bulls and behave like pit bulls, and, as with pit bulls, your best bet is to not move too suddenly, not raise your voice and not make eye contact.

But, like I said, I've only ever been on the outside looking in.

Blackmer, you see, is a community divided along racial lines, a mixture of two groups that don't tend to mix—the remnants of the Okies who came to work the fields three generations ago, then moved up or at least moved on, and the Hispanics who have been working the fields ever since.

Racism, in a town like this, just is. We're animals, and when we're penned with animals that have different colorings and markings, the males of the species are going to get nervous. You're going to hear a chorus of growling, and we're going to bare our teeth and raise our hackles and occasionally try to rip the throats out of the alien creatures.

But then, maybe I'm dead wrong. Maybe a racial utopia is possible. After all, the hardest Mexican gangster I ever met had a ghost-white complexion and pale blue eyes.

I had known Owen Ferguson, or known of him, for most of my life. It made sense he would insinuate himself in this because he knew both me and Rich and had never liked us. I could just see him in a murky, smoke-filled living room in some little back-alley house, vacuuming up a line off the communal mirror, then glancing around at his red-eyed associates and saying in that nasal voice of his, "Yeah, I know that guy, Sam Schuler. He's a punk, aye. I'll go hit 'im up an' he'll just fork over the money, man. Don't even sweat it."

The joke we used to make was that Owen Ferguson was like Tarzan, raised among the apes and then gone on to lead them. When I entered Conejo Junior High I was surprised to discover this homely white boy was the toughest kid on campus. Most of us Caucasian youths had to tread lightly, to stake out our territory at the corner of the grounds and endure the sneers and scoffs and Spanish insults we couldn't understand. But not Owen Ferguson. He was one of them. He lived in the middle of gangland, had a Mexican stepfather and a half-Mexican half-brother, and he had run wild in the dirtiest streets and alleyways of Blackmer his entire life, until his English was spoken like a second language and he sneered and scoffed at white people and thought of them as a separate species from himself.

Even then, at twelve, Owen had been lanky and rangy, half a head taller than most of his friends. And he was already renowned as a fighter—always willing, eager, desperate to square off and start swinging with anyone, any time. He was a tyrant on the school grounds, holding court at a blue fiberglass picnic table, "talking shit" with a Mexican accent among the budding twelve-year-old Hispanic thugs whose big brothers and uncles and fathers were the veteran criminals and warriors of Blackmer. Even then, Owen was already a *vato* in his soul and a favorite of the *vatos* in his neighborhood despite his blue-eyed, raw-boned, ridge runner ancestry.

That he would come for me seemed inevitable. As Sully had pointed out, Owen "lived" just across the parking lot. He and his crew had made a sort of clubhouse of the bar off the side of Rancho Bonita, the Mexican restaurant that was just a two-minute walk from where I now stood.

I tried to imagine reasoning with him, explaining what had happened and seeing his eyes soften with comprehension, but I shook my head and cursed. He didn't have the capacity. The arc of his evolution had been completed in junior high.

I figured the worst was going to happen and tried to brace myself for it.

THREE

When I saw Owen entering the store about a half-hour before closing, my body stopped being mine. My legs went rubbery, the room seemed to tilt and swing around like a carnival ride, and I couldn't do a thing except stand there and stare.

Up to that point I had succeeded in putting it out of my mind. I had to write a report on a hundred-year-old novel called *The Octopus* for my class on local history and I was trying to force the story down in huge gulps, to take it like medicine—and was surprised to find myself enjoying it. The evil thing lingered just outside the spotlight of my thoughts, and every so often I would look up and think about Rich getting his head split open with a blackjack, but I had made up my mind not to fall to panic until I knew for certain that there was something to panic about. I was almost ready to sigh relief, at least for tonight, when the electric sensor on the door sounded and I marked my place with my forefinger, lifted my eyes, and felt my heart clench to a stop.

Under the fluorescents Owen Ferguson's crisp white T-shirt shimmered, his loose khaki pants were pressed and new. His hair was mowed tight to the scalp, darkening the top of a long, insect-looking head that was dented and scarred from his uncountable street fights. The overall effect of him was clean and utilitarian, but somehow disposable. Cheap. The only blemish on his appearance was the line of dark green cursive tattooed at a crooked angle on his neck, under his right ear.

My mouth fell open and I said, "Hey…" Nothing else occurred to me. Owen's face showed only that slack, somehow demented look of a person whose mind is steel-reinforced against fear. I wondered if he could jump out of a tenth-story window and never change that dead-faced expression all the way down to earth. He had tight, thin lips, close-set eyes and a smattering of freckles over the bridge of his nose.

I couldn't move as he drew close. I just blinked ahead, cleared my throat and tried to find words that might save me. I didn't even flinch when he didn't break stride and sprang forward and socked me under my left eye. I didn't fall either. I guess my head just snapped over and then back like my neck was a spring.

"What do you think, bitch?" he said.

I blinked at him. I still had the paperback in my hand,

closed on my finger as if I was going to go back to reading. My other hand, I realized, was now holding my face.

"You think it's over or what? You think you and your faggot friend can pull that shit and then you don't gotta pay?" He sounded a little like Marlon Brando. His voice seemed to be generated in his nasal passages and he had a painful-looking under-bite that you didn't notice until he spoke.

"Look, man." It was a strangled, distant version of my voice. "I didn't—"

His hand slapped the glass lottery ticket display that was built into the counter. "*Shut* the fuck up! You know what I'm talking about. You know me, right?" He pointed at his own chest. "You know what I'll *do*, Homes. You heard about your buddy. I'm gonna be outside." He seemed to think a moment. "Five hundred bucks," he said, drilling me with his look. "And don't give me no stories. You got it in *there*." He jabbed a finger at the cash register.

"Aw, no man, I can't—"

He froze me with another look, his bulldog jaw a challenge, his eyes like little blue pools of congealed gel, his whole head like a wax sculpture some kids had played football with. "Who the fuck you kidding, Homes?" he said. "You think I don't know what happens in this fucking place? You're a fucking thief already so don't even try to blow smoke up my ass."

"I'll lose my job!" I was fighting the whine that wanted to creep into my voice. "I didn't take anybody's fucking weed, man. I don't know what you heard but it's bullshit."

His eyebrows shot up his forehead. His pupils were small as pinpricks in the faded blue irises, but those tiny spots seemed to be pouring forth animosity. He couldn't believe, evidently, that we were still having this conversation. "Try me," he said. "Just try me, motherfucker. I want you to." And he stepped backward and finally released me from his glare, turned around and glided away over the maroon utility mats. I watched him exit the bright store and stride into the nighttime parking lot toward his lowered, black-windowed Celica.

I felt like I had entered a dream state. I found myself moving with the studied deliberateness of a drunk. My hand rattled as I marked my place in *The Octopus* with a register receipt and laid it on the shelf under the counter, beside the basket of matches. I stared down for a moment, concentrating on breathing, then forced myself to move. I went into the walk-in cooler to throw some beer onto the shelves and create the impression I had done some work tonight. There was no one in the store and while I was back there I half-hoped that Owen would come in, lean over the counter and hit NO SALE and grab all the cash he wanted. But I knew it wasn't going to happen. I had to submit. It was a street-dominance ritual.

Everyone who worked here stole from this place, and Owen knew it. Hell, half the town knew it. But nobody stole five hundred bucks in one shot, and I sure wasn't going to risk my job, kill the goose that laid golden eggs, just to give it to this semi-literate fucking cretin for something I didn't do.

So where did that leave me?

I could fight him, I guessed. I even thought I could win if I really wanted to. He was a couple of inches taller than me, but I had twenty pounds of muscle on him. I had wrestled in high school—senior year I was second place in the county in my weight division—and the three drunken fights I had been in since then were decided by my ability to maul and pin my opponent. I began to imagine myself "shooting the legs," taking Owen to the ground, twisting him up and holding him paralyzed, but then I shook my head. I may win the battle, but did I think the guy fought by any rules? Did I think he wasn't armed? I was practically guaranteed a bullet through the neck or a switchblade buried in my kidney.

No, what I knew I had to do was let him sock me a few times, knock me down, and then let him pull out my wallet and get the thirty bucks in there and call me "pussy" and "bitch." And then maybe he'd let it go. There was a chance, anyway.

I came out of the walk-in cooler and went to the breaker box and flipped the green-painted breaker switches, darkening the store. I had pulled the newspaper display in at nine. I crossed the shadowy room and locked the door, leaving the keys dangling in the slot. With the illumination inside the store gone I could see Owen's car in the empty parking lot, a high lot-lamp shedding dull whiteness down on it, and I could hear the faint thump of rap music. He was parked right next to my Fairlane. This thing was going to happen. I went behind the counter, punched in the code so the register popped the cash drawer and started grinding out its report, and I started gathering the cash from the compartments. I tore off the three feet of register tape and took that and the cash into the back to count up and fill out the closing sheet. When I was done I bound it all up with a rubber band, put the package in the floor safe and spun the dial with a determined twist of my wrist, locking all the money away from myself and Owen.

I stood straight and realized this was it. I took a deep breath. Fuck it. I'd do it. Face the music and all that. I stepped out of the back and I blinked and my mouth dropped open. I pulled a sharp breath and said, "What the fuck." There was a black and white cop car nosed up behind Owen's Toyota—and my Fairlane—in the otherwise empty parking lot. Owen was out, ass against the back corner of his car, and a big cop was passing a flashlight beam over the seats through the open driver's door. Owen appeared bored. Then his head turned and he seemed to look right at me.

I stood there. I waited a full minute while the cop harassed the thug, and then they had some parting words and Owen got in his car and the cop got in his. The cop seemed to wait for Owen to start the Celica, back out and begin crawling away, and then the black and white slid along behind him. The parking lot was empty except for my Fairlane—a white, used-up junkyard relic waiting off to the side, leaking its nightly puddle of 10-40 onto the asphalt.

I didn't know what to make of what had just happened except I was certain it wasn't good. Cops interrupting anything short of a child-murder is never good, but there was something especially horrifying about this. I punched in the code with a trembling hand, activating the alarm, and got out of the store. No headlights appeared. Nobody bothered me as I walked to my car.

The only other remarkable thing about this night was that as I slowed to turn into my apartment complex a pair of headlights swelled up close to the back of my car, as if the driver was trying to tell me something, and then their motor bellowed and the car bore hard to the left and careened away. I couldn't see if it was Owen's Toyota, but I assumed it wasn't, because Owen would have kindly followed me in and worked me over in the dark parking lot. Just some tough local gorilla beating his chest. At least that's what I told myself.

FOUR

When I went into Vanguard the next day Sully was behind the counter. He had a knot of hangers-on around, a couple of white skaters with the backward caps, tattoos and eyebrow piercings and a tiny Americanized Mexican who must have been nearing forty, clinging to the group until he could score something for free. They had a football game on the TV that was mounted up in the corner, over the magazine rack, and you could bet the business was losing a hundred bucks in beer and cigarettes today.

I walked in and said, "Hey," and they all looked at me. A couple of the guys muttered greetings and Sully averted his eyes and echoed, "Hey."

I stuffed my jacket on a shelf under the counter and got an orange juice from one of the coolers. Sully eyed his friends. "Guys," he said. "Go wait at my car. I'll catch up."

They made a few cracks but did as he said, and when they were gone Sully looked hard at me. "You fucked up, dude." His voice was low and grave. Secretive. His brown eyes hooked mine and held them fast. In the naked daylight his face looked like it had been boiled until the flesh was ready to drop off his skull.

"What?" I felt the ice trickling down my spine, raising gooseflesh on the backs of my arms. I had a good, sickening idea *what*.

"Calling the fucking cops."

"That shit last night? Hey man, I didn't call the cops. They just *showed up*. Owen needs to know that. Can you tell him? Tell someone who knows him? Do me a favor and do that, can you?" My voice was strained. Terror was knocking hard.

"Yeah," Sully said. "I'll call him, dude. But he's pissed. He was in here saying all kinds of shit. I'm just telling you. Next time I see that guy, if I was you? I would call the cops."

And that began the longest eight hours I had ever known. Like they say, the hardest part is the not knowing. How about not knowing if you're gonna get shot or stabbed or blackjacked or what? How about terror shutting down your mind a hundred times in a night as you wait for some skinny murderous prick to come and rush you every time you hear the electronic buzzer in the doorway, every time you see a lowered car pull up thumping rap music? How about thinking every tough, wannabe pimp asshole—the guys who made up half of Vanguard's clientele—was sent by Owen and his crowd, and he's going to maybe rush you and drag you over the counter, or maybe just whip out a gun and start blasting away?

That was my eight hours and in case I was going to forget my predicament, at seven-thirty Rich came in, still alive after all. He wasn't so bad. He just looked like his head had been dynamited to small pieces and then stuck back together by a six-year-old using Elmer's glue. He displayed, with an odd pride, the gap where one of his big front teeth was gone and the other broken in half, under a purple lip that was completely split, four or five times its normal size and sewed back together with thick black thread. One eye was puffed shut, his nose ballooned and squishy-looking, and his cheeks and forehead dark and lumpy.

"What happened to you?" I blurted. "I mean, I know what happened, but do you have to come up with money?"

"Yeah, dude. But you know me. Blood from a fuckin' turnip. Fuck those guys. I'm making myself scarce. I'm going to fuckin' Canada, dude."

"Canada?" I grabbed Marlboros off the counter display and set them in front of him and he picked them up, started tapping the pack against his palm and said, "Thanks, bro."

"You ought to stick around, man," I said. "Owen's due by here any minute to fuckin' kill me."

"Dude!" He became hushed and serious, and glanced behind him, looking for Owen. "I heard about that! Fuck, why'd you call the cops on him?"

My heart sank. I explained myself to Rich, emphatically, as if he could help me. I guess the logic was that he could start spreading the rumor the other way, telling the right people—or people who might tell the right people—that I was a hundred percent victim of circumstance.

"That's fucked up," Rich said, amusement breaking through, glad that his turn was over and that for all his stupidity he wasn't in as deep as me. Then he looked away and looked back. "What time you get outta here?"

I frowned. No way I was getting pulled into the orbit of Rich's idiocy—ever again, I had decided—but I said, "Ten, just like always."

"Oh." He knitted his brows, not asking me to hang out after all. "Hey, you think I can get one more pack for my driver? I'll pay you for it."

I looked out and saw a little red Japanese go-cart with gray primer on the fender. I couldn't make out the driver but he was no friend of mine and I didn't need to give him smokes. "Pay me when?"

Rich looked at me and I could see him trying to do something cute with that wrecked face. "I'll gladly pay you Tuesday for some Marlboros today."

I suddenly felt like throwing something at him, yelling, kicking him in the ass and chasing him off. "No way, man. You already owe for a dozen packs. Share the ones you got, asshole."

I saw something like surprise, maybe even anger, flicker in his good eye and then vanish. "Yeah, you're right. Sorry. Well, I'll send you a postcard from Canada, bro. Hey, thanks for the smokes. Seriously."

He was retreating as he spoke and then he was gone. I watched the little Japanese car pull away, the weight of my impending doom settling onto my thoughts again. And then I slapped the countertop. I had forgotten to find out what had become of the pound of weed. Jesus, that could get us off the hook! I hustled out to the parking lot to wave them down, but they had already driven out of sight.

During the minutes before closing it got worse, not better. It wasn't the home stretch, it was the danger zone; the handiest time to get me. It was so intense that when I finally found myself driving away with the store locked behind me, I started laughing a strange laugh that I had never experienced before. Nothing at all was funny, but I guess that tension simply must escape. I grinned and I started thinking that maybe, maybe it would all blow over now. Sully must have gotten hold of Owen, and maybe I was granted some kind of reprieve in some goofy-ass court of coked-up gangsters. It was going to be fine.

The door to our apartment was unlocked when I got home. I didn't panic then, but I stepped in quick and said, "Jill?"

There was no answer.

I closed the door, my heart picking up tempo. Nobody was in the living room but the bathroom door was closed with the stripe of light under it, so I didn't think much about anything yet. When I walked into our bedroom, I stopped and blinked, completely dumbfounded. The bed was not just unmade, the blanket and top sheet were ripped away, drooling onto the floor, leaving the fitted sheet totally exposed. Three of our four pillows were mashed against the headboard. The fourth was obviously on the floor on my side of the bed where I couldn't see it. We had matching bedside lamps and the one on Jill's side was on the floor. Beside it was a pair of her panties.

I stared for a long moment, feeling the way you feel when you're looking at books in the warm safe environment of the library and you come across those old pictures of war atrocities or hollow-eyed, skeletal prisoners in death camps gazing frankly at the camera. What I was seeing wouldn't fit into my understanding of reality. It disturbed me on a level I couldn't have prepared for. I had a weird thought of Jill screwing someone else on our bed, and me coming home while they were halfway into it, but I knew that was impossible.

"Jill?" My voice was louder and shrill, and I was up against the bathroom door now. I rapped three times and said, "Jill!" then rapped again.

The toilet flushed. I heard rustling, feet on the floor, and the latch clicked and the door came open.

She was naked.

"I need…to take a shower," she said. Her face was

bloodless and without expression, her eyes huge and empty.

"What? Jill! Look at me." I took her shoulders. There was a bruise on her neck, the size of a thumbprint. I already knew. "Did someone come in here?"

"They…they *knocked*," she said, and took a huge breath, as if thinking of it exhausted her. "There were two of them. A white guy and a-a-another guy, and they just backed me in there." She glanced at the bedroom.

I think I said "No!" but maybe I didn't. There was a humming growing in my ears, speckles in my vision, and I might have rolled my eyes up in my head and passed out if Jill hadn't started crying.

It was just a sniffle at first, but it brought me back like smelling salts, made me smart with the knowledge of who the goddamned victim was here. She was starting to shake, and I reached out, pulled her against me and began rubbing the silky planes of her back and telling her everything was all right.

But even then, a blinding rage, a need to do something, was clouding my thinking. We were going to the police. Modern investigative techniques would turn the motherfuckers up and I would arm myself, go into the courtroom during their trial and execute them. Right through the face. The cops could drag me away after that. I didn't give a fuck.

"We have to go to the police," I said into her hair, my voice sounding thin, almost metallic. "Go to the doctor, do all that."

"There's nothing!" she sobbed into my shoulder. "Sam, they had on ski masks." And lower, she said, "The even used rubbers. All I could tell, the first guy, he was white, and the other guy was dark. Mexican—probably."

And it came to me. Hit me so hard I felt the breath go out of me. Owen Ferguson. Oh Christ, he had given up on getting me at the liquor store but that guy wouldn't just give up altogether, would he? How could I not know that he would teach me, one way or another, what happens when some punk crosses him? My body felt so hot it might begin steaming. My rage was suddenly corrupted by guilt and the combination was so poisonous my knees were buckling.

"Jill, I think—"

"Sam?" Her voice was thick with crying now, tinged with hysterics, and it took her a couple of times to get it out. "I want you to take...I want to go...to my *mom's*!" And with the last word she began sobbing too hard to speak.

"Okay," I said. "Okay, Jill."

I nearly had to carry her into the bedroom to get her dressed.

We were mostly silent and Jill didn't seem to want to be touched on the drive. All I could think about was Owen, but I couldn't bring myself to put any of it into words. I tried to comfort her a couple of times but wound up stammering and rambling, promising again and again that we were going to move out of the apartment, we were going to move far away from Blackmer.

Her mom answered the door, looking like hell. The woman was a waitress with a raspy voice and bleached gray hair. She was long divorced from Jill's father and remarried to a tough little Filipino biker. They lived at the end of a cul-de-sac in a tiny, grubby house that smelled of their pugs, Vinnie and Minnie, and their cigarette smoke. I hadn't phoned ahead. I walked Jill to the door and delivered her inside. She kept saying, "I'm fine now. I'm fine," as we went up the darkened walkway. She seemed a little irritated with me but I didn't dwell on it and went ahead with my duty. I began trying to explain to her mother, saying, "Two guys…they…they came into our place…" my speech halting idiotically until Jill threw me a look and recited the basic facts in an eerily tranquil voice.

I assumed her mother would get her through the police and medical stuff, and was ashamed at how glad I was to be avoiding it. As soon as I could I began inching toward the door, saying, "Listen, I got some stuff to do."

Jill sat at the dining room table, which was a few feet from the front door. She didn't look disappointed or hurt by the idea of my leaving. She didn't even seem to hear me. Her mother glanced at the clock and said, "I hope you don't have any stupid ideas, Sam!"

I said, "No, no, I don't," and slipped out the door, my heart pounding, pulling the cool night air into my lungs like I'd been suffocating. I made it to my car in the damp dark evening, in that sleeping, ugly, lower-class neighborhood, relishing the solitude, reveling in the sudden silence, relaxing with the momentary relief from the high, tense feedback of misery emanating from Jill.

But it was a false calm. I was a momentary escapee, hugging myself against a tree in the midnight woods, catching my breath as the hounds barked and bayed and closed distance behind me. And I was sprinting again in no time, charging ahead into this new wilderness of troubles, this waking nightmare, and knowing it couldn't turn out any way but fucked.

FIVE

I kept the Fairlane at seventy-five along the deserted highway and got off at the familiar exit back in Blackmer. Mist was visible under the street lamps. The red traffic lights blinked over the deserted intersections. Thick clouds drifted in front of a full white moon like the backdrop in a vampire movie. I rolled into Baron Square and parked next to Rancho Bonita, the Mexican place across from Vanguard, and did something for which I should be dead.

How do you explain this? I guess it's what guys do in war. They march *into* fire when everything in them shrieks to turn and run, to dive for cover, to cry and beg God or the enemy or fate to spare them. But they tromp onward with the bullets streaking past, blowing heads apart and snapping into chests and limbs, with bombs detonating and their friends doubling over, disemboweled, screaming, in little pieces. And at the end of it they're either dead, they wish they were dead, or they're appalled by their own ridiculous luck.

My palm hit the worn, metal plate and the door swung open. It was after one a.m. in the middle of the week and the barroom was alive in a slow, dark way like a welter of snakes in the bottom of a pit.

It was a small bar with a small stage in the corner where local bands and karaoke outfits set up a few times a week. The walls were spotted with the usual neon, relief tins from beer companies, and framed pictures meant to add character. There was a tropical Mexican motif, with a few clay parrots painted in primary colors and standing in metal rings suspended from the ceiling, and there was a shitty mural along the far wall that might have been painted by a ten-year-old, depicting a beach, blue skies and some palm trees.

As I stepped in I caught a glimpse of myself in a big wall mirror. I was all wrong here. There was no hazy smile floating on my face, no trickle of noisy, happy nonsense on my lips. My mouth was mashed to a thin line, my nostrils spread, my eyes banged open so the irises were like holes punched in the dough of my face.

I grimaced, tore my gaze away and scanned the fifteen-odd patrons. The obnoxious thumping and ranting from the corner speakers was black gangsta rap, the partiers were mostly Mexican with a couple of white wannabe gangsters in the mix and a couple of slutty white girls drinking and leering off in a corner. I knew I stood out in this ethnic, urban atmosphere. I looked like I belonged in Del Mar with the surfers and college kids. My heart was kicking like an animal trapped inside my chest cavity and it kicked harder with every step. But something in me had ruled out turning back. I would walk right into enemy fire. It was all I had tonight.

I recognized Owen's buzz-cut, evilly shaped cranium from across the room. He had his back to the bar, around its far curve, so his back was toward me when I spotted him. As I approached I saw the side of his face and heard snatches of his nasally voice. He was smirking and jabbering with his outthrust lower jaw, pint of beer in hand, amid the scariest collection of macho, dangerous gangsters you'd ever want to see; belligerent, loud, arrogant Mexican-Americans with thick, powerful builds and huge shirts and baggy pants; young men who had lost their youth, hanging with an air of drug-smoke, marked up with haphazard tattoos barely visible against their muddy skin, their dog-like hair cropped down to close black mats on their sloping skulls.

I stepped toward them. Nobody was looking at me and I almost stopped, realizing the enemy hadn't even opened fire yet—I could just sneak away, live to fight another day and all that. But then Owen's gaze locked with mine as if he had been waiting for me. Something shifted behind his eyes, utter confusion and surprise, and then the veil of stone-cold killer-cool dropped over his face again and it was like that flash of humanity had never been there.

I was standing three feet away. My hearing was clouded by blood pressure. The rap music and drunk conversations seemed like something off in the distance, the whole world a TV with the volume turned down. Everything seemed to have fallen away except the battered, malignant face of Owen Ferguson. He was wearing a loose, checkered, button-down shirt that looked right off the rack and he was holding a fresh pint of piss-colored beer at chest level. The Mexicans around him had gone silent, looking at me like they might explode to action and kill me any second.

"You fucking stupid, Homes, or what?" Owen said in his jaw-sprung, perpetual Brando imitation.

I found my voice wasn't quite there. I wasn't quite angry or high on adrenaline; all I had was the theoretical knowledge that I *ought* to be angry, that I *ought* to feel like killing, but I was deep inside my shell.

I nodded and said, "Yeah, I'm fucking stupid," so quiet I could hardly hear myself, and Owen watched, completely dumbfounded as my hand reached out and tipped his pint glass into his chin, washing the amber liquid down the front of his button-down shirt. I did it with my left hand, and I managed to square off during everyone's collective gasp and immediately snap a punch into his cheek with my right. I had the satisfaction of seeing him cower against the bar, squinch his face and cover up with his hands for a split second, and I stepped back and elevated my fists in a silly boxer's pose.

"Let's do it, bitch!" I said, so loud that the entire room

stopped dead and watched. "Come on, you faggot rapist piece of shit! Bring it, motherfucker!" I heard my speech tinged with the pseudo-black street dialect the gangsters use and I had no idea where it came from. The action had cracked me out of my shell and I was suddenly a stranger to myself.

There were four of Owen's friends mere inches away, but I was guessing Owen would need to rescue his reputation by personally beating me, at which point I would beat him—to death if I could. That was the plan that I hadn't articulated to myself. That's what had brought me here, and that's what I was expecting to happen when the plug was pulled on my consciousness.

I learned later, of course, that one of the big Mexicans had simply set his feet and slammed a fist into the side of my head and then it had been basketball shoes, boots and fists striking me like bricks swung on the end of ropes.

The bartender was a youngish Romeo-type with his hair slicked back from his widow's peak and his chest hair coming out of his open collar. Maybe he recognized me as one of the clerks at Vanguard, or maybe he would have done the same for anyone, but he saved me, yelling, "Hey! Hey! I'm calling the cops! Knock it the fuck off right now!" as the gangsters stomped on me or bent down to land punches. I heard all this later, from the bartender himself, after I woke up to the sound of sirens. He actually did call the cops and even scampered around the bar, phone in hand, yelling and warding my attackers off, telling them there was a room full of witnesses. They had finally listened to him and hustled out and roared off in their lowered cars.

As I crawled up to a stool it felt like half my face had been torn off. My fingers explored the parts of it that were bigger and squishier and sorer, and the parts of it that were split open. I needed ice and maybe stitches. The inside of my lip was shredded. At least one tooth was loose. My left thigh had a cruel cramp stitched into it and my left arm, around the elbow, felt either sprained or broken.

Two cops strolled in—the big one who had harassed Owen last night, and a smaller one with a mustache. They were both white. They sat at a table with me, two scrubbed healthy faces, two cropped scalps and black outfits, their crowded tool belts and bullet-proof vests making them stiff and awkward in sitting positions. The bartender worked with one ear cocked toward us. I told the cops I had no idea who had done it. Bunch of Mexicans, I said. My own fault, I said. I had a few drinks too many and I mouthed off and swung first.

That was good enough for the cops, and they radioed it in as "mutual combat" and left, telling me I might want to get myself to the emergency room.

Last call had come and gone by then and the place was empty. The bartender put both hands on the bar when the door shut behind the cops. He had big, glassy black eyes and the typical Latino caterpillar mustache sitting on his thick upper lip. He said, "That was smart, bro. You don't want to rat on those guys. I was you, I'd go home and pack and leave town right now."

I thanked him for his advice through my damaged mouth and I dragged myself out. There was nobody waiting for me in the parking lot. I made it to my car and went home, but I didn't pack and leave town.

SIX

My cousin Tommy had spent good portions of his life in county, state and federal lockups. He was well into his forties and usually had half a dozen girlfriends waiting in the wings that he liked to brag about but didn't like anyone to actually see.

When I was a kid his girlfriends looked like TV stars. They were wholesome or sleazy or somewhere in between; they were sprightly and high-breasted or busty and hippy or somewhere in between; they were blonde or brunette or redheaded or some mixed shade. But they were always something to look at. They never rated any lower than an eight-point-five, and it seemed they'd do anything for him. The last I'd heard, Tommy had made me eight second cousins by five different women.

But as the years went on his girlfriends became rougher, tougher, sleazier, shadier, older, meaner, fatter and generally lower on the attractiveness scale until Tommy left them at home, snuck over and fucked them when he needed to, strung them along, used them for their cars or food stamps or drugs, and then casually strolled out of their lives when they had a fit of self-respect and started screaming at him.

Tommy was still the cool character he had been from maybe 1982 to maybe 1996, but he was trapped in an aging husk. Time had carved lines into his face, bled the gold from his hair and laid a layer of grizzle around his middle. He was still a presence; still a big, loud, powerful, vaguely gorilla-looking shape, but none of the dewy young girls who made him antsy would look his way anymore. He knew this but if you spent any time around him you would never know he knew it.

I thought of Tommy the next day as I awoke alone in the apartment Jill and I shared. I had slept, or tried to sleep, on the couch in the little living room and I lay there staring at the ceiling as the dawn became morning outside. I was sore all over. I had leaned in front of the bathroom mirror, gasped at myself, but determined that I didn't need stitches. My face was just well tenderized. And I had heard that a tooth knocked loose would set again if left in its hole, so I did just that. When I walked back from the bathroom I could feel where each foot or fist had dug into my torso and limbs, but nothing was so smashed that the pain wouldn't fade. Or so I guessed.

Owen and his "boyz," it seemed, hadn't had quite enough time to work.

I thought of a lot of things as I lay there, in the little living room Jill had decorated and spent so much time with me in. I thought of the past, of my childhood, of what I believed I was and how all of that had turned out to be a cheap facade. I thought that if I let this thing slither away into yesterday, and then last week, and then a month ago, without grabbing onto it, without taking hold of it and mastering it—or at least making my best attempt—I would be looking back on it with shame for the rest of my life.

And so the little footpath of my thoughts wound around and brought me to Tommy again. Some people have friends on the police force or local government. Some can pay high-powered attorneys to start the wheels of so-called justice turning to draw in and grind up their enemies. In my hour of need, when I was confronted with my own impotence, I could only think of Tommy.

He was as soft-hearted in his own way as he was malicious and self-serving. He was a street kid who my aunt hadn't wanted or cared about, and who had raised himself in the city, fighting and cheating and winning from his earliest childhood. It left him a compulsive hustler and, like every one of this breed, it had cultivated in him rare talents. He was vastly intelligent, with surprising imagination and lighting wit, but the spinning gears were set too far apart, never meshing, never taking him anywhere. He had never had a steady job that I was aware of but he worked relentlessly, seven days a week, scavenging scraps of other people's wealth, foraging like a wolf, swindling fortunes and waking each morning with nothing again.

And there was another side of him, a vicious Mr. Hyde that emerged when the fast talk and the smiles and lies had failed. Tommy was dangerous. A big man with quick, fluid strength who had spent half his life in cages with other desperate and angry human males. He had bragged to me when he was drunk that he had never lost a fight. "And that," he said, "ain't on the fuckin' playground, Sammy. I'm talkin' in the worst places in the world with the toughest motherfuckers in the world."

None of it left him much of a human being, but it left him with a specialized set of skills. And this morning, as I washed up and burned on this sandbar, as I marshaled my energies and prepared to croak for help, he was the only person I could make out in the distance.

He answered his cell phone by saying, "This is Tom."

"Tommy," I said. I was sitting up on the couch. Morning light was pouring in the front window. I had the phone against my head and his cell number, scribbled on a scrap of paper months ago, sitting on my knee.

"Who's this?"

"Tommy, it's Sam, your cousin. Listen—"

"You sound like shit, kid."

"Yeah. Hey, I need to talk to you about some stuff. Can you meet me somewhere?"

"Sure. Well, shit. Can you come get me? My car ain't running."

I had the immediate thought that his car was running just fine, but he was working some angle—maybe just trying to save gas, for fuck's sake. "Yeah. You still out there by the beach?"

"Yeah, but, fuck…"

So I ended up arranging to meet him by the Amoco station out on Highway 1. Like everything with him, there was a story that didn't add up explaining why he couldn't drive and why I couldn't pick him up at wherever his current home was. Something about a new place that was hard to find, a bitchy old lady, a dangerous dog. I spaced out while he delivered his spiel. I didn't give a fuck.

When he got into my car, for the first time in my life, the guy seemed speechless. He looked at my face in the harsh ten a.m. light and said, "What the fuck…" and that was it for several seconds. He reached out and took my chin in thick, grease-stained fingers, turned my head and pursed his lips, furrowed his brow like a mother contemplating her sick child.

"You fall into the tiger cage at the zoo?"

"Something like that. I need to get some stuff," I said. "A gun, I think."

This was supposed to raise the question of why the fuck I, his relatively clean-cut cousin, would need a gun. This was supposed to awaken his sense of family honor and make him vow to never rest until I had been avenged. But he wasn't biting. His large, blue, once-attractive eyes stared right through me a moment and then he said, "You got money?"

"A little in the bank, not much but—"

"Never mind." He waved his hand. "We can get some."

Tommy practically ignored me. I was merely a sounding board for his bullshit. He was off and running on his hustle. He only discussed his plan to "get funds"—which was simply to make me steal a chainsaw.

He knew the guy who possessed the chainsaw— "owned" might be too strong a word here—and some deal had gone bad that Tommy wanted to set straight, maybe; I still don't know with any certainty. But they knew his car in this neighborhood, and he might have been spotted doing this himself, so he had rifled the mental files, done some kind of calculation and decided me needing something presented him with an opportunity to even up with this guy.

Tommy got out of the passenger's seat and we switched places. He was dressed in clothes that had lost their bloom, a crusty leather jacket with a blue sweatshirt hood hanging over the collar, loose-fit jeans that were still new and wanted to be nice but had become grease-spotted while Tommy tinkered with stolen bikes or made quick adjustments to idling engines. His hair was longish, but not long, washing out from dark blond to gray. Tommy was once extraordinarily handsome and his face, when I bothered to consider it, made me give the amused grunt you give when you see an aging starlet. The striking, bright-eyed kid from those early publicity photos is still there, but distorted, transformed by the wicked workings of time, and the starlet just looks that much more pathetic as she tries to drape herself in the glamour of the old days. That was Tommy, except he was a little too scary to be pathetic.

As he walked around the hood of the Fairlane he slipped on wraparound sunglasses—right in style, circa 1990—and pulled the sweatshirt hood up so he looked like the Unibomber. We climbed in on opposite sides and I watched as he settled his large gorilla frame into the driver's seat.

He pursed his lips, orienting himself to the gear lever on the steering column. "Good old three-on-the-tree," he said. "This got the four-twenty-seven?"

"Yeah."

"You want to get rid of this thing, lemme know. I know a guy loves these fucking cars."

"Maybe after today," I said, "When it's known by the police."

He threw me a mirror-lensed glance and said, "Don't go gettin' nervous on me now, honey, when you got me all hard and ready."

"Jesus," I said. "Stop."

He turned the key, listened to the motor and revved it up to a snarling scream a couple of times. "Don't worry. I'll snuggle you afterward, Sammy-boy!" He braced both arms against the steering wheel as he popped the clutch.

The tires screeched as the V-8 yanked us forward and flung us out of the Amoco lot. Tommy said, "That's what I'm talkin' about!" as we fishtailed, kicking up gravel at the edge of the road and then grabbing the pavement and rocketing onto the freeway. My stomach lurched, the engine yowled higher and higher until I thought it was going to shatter, and he finally punched the clutch and shifted into second when we were doing forty.

We rolled into the poor side of Blackmer ten minutes later. It was a nice day for robbing houses. The blue sky was only marked with a couple of fading chemtrails, the sun was flexing and a friendly breeze sprinkled the dandelion seeds across the ragged lawns.

I did just as he said, and just as he said, there was nobody home. Maybe Tommy had killed the guy last week and he was rotting inside the place. Who knew? We backed into the driveway of a gray-white house with a front yard of dirt and a layer of grime on the windows. It was located behind another house. Someone's rental unit. The operation took five minutes. I got out and let myself in the side gate, limped to the backyard, and went to the old rust-rotted hardware-store tin shed Tommy had described. It wasn't locked, and when the door opened daylight fell on the big orange Husqvarna chainsaw Tommy had described.

"That's a goddamned thousand-dollar piece of equipment!" Tommy said as we drove away. The chainsaw was on the backseat. It looked brand new and it was huge, although it had been unexpectedly light as I carried it out. Tommy was agitated now, high, drugged by the success of the caper. "Motherfucker stole it from *me*," he said as he drove. "Sneaky prick didn't think I'd come take it back 'cause he called the cops when I beat his ass. That thing better still run."

I just looked at him, still donning his Unibomber shades and hood. I was unable to discern what the reality of the situation might have been. Who knew who stole what from whom in the circles Tommy moved in?

"Where we going now?" I said.

We were wandering from the residence I had just robbed, cruising the neighborhoods of Blackmer, working our way out of the homely, poverty-ridden streets to where lawnmower wheels left geometrically perfect stripes in the front yards; where the sidewalks were uncluttered and uncracked and the cars clean and new. Tommy rolled down the window as he lit a cigarette, speaking out the side of his mouth, impersonating what was probably supposed to be a Texas tycoon. "I'm gonna show you how we do things in the big league, son! Market conditions are favorable to sell at a profit this morning!"

"What, you gonna pawn that thing?"

"Shhh! You hear that?" Tommy had his left ear cocked toward the window, he plucked the cigarette from his mouth and said, "That's oppor*toon*ity knockin', boy!"

I listened. I heard a small engine grinding away somewhere.

"Yep, that's us," he said in his own voice again, pushing

the gas and listening for the source of the noise. "Watch this, Sam. Just watch this. Wetbacks always got cold hard fuckin' cash!"

He listened as he drove, smoking rapidly in his excitement, and finally turned the car around a bend, and said, "Oh yeah. They're the ones."

Before us, against the curb in front of a house with fresh paint, professional landscape design and a deep green lawn, there was a well-outfitted gardening rig. I looked at the new metal trailer loaded with equipment and the big white Ford truck in front of it, and I began to get the idea.

Tommy pulled up behind the truck, set the brake and turned off the car. He flipped his sweatshirt hood down and smoothed his hair, then got out and walked up to the house. After a moment he got the attention of a skinny, dark Mexican who was running a weed-eater. I heard Tommy shout something about a *"patrone"* a few times and the guy shut his machine off and went to the back yard. Tommy fidgeted and glanced up and down the street for a few seconds, until a boss-type emerged.

The boss was maybe forty, Mexican but Americanized. Thick and frog-shaped with the black caterpillar on his upper lip and an intensely skeptical glint in his eye.

I watched them approach the car. I just sat in the front seat, seeing myself and Tommy through this workingman's eyes and feeling like something he had noticed in the uncut grass, left behind by a dog.

"That thing's brand-new!" Tommy said. I had a view

of the two men's middle-aged midsections out the car's window and I saw Tommy's hands shape his thoughts as he spoke. "You gotta cut a tree down, this mother'll go through a fuckin' giant redwood like warm fuckin' butter!"

"I already got a chainsaw," the Mexican said in flat American.

I heard Tommy scoff. "What do you got? A fourteen-inch for chomping up trimmings?"

"That's right."

"What're you gonna do to a tree with that fuckin' toy? Hurt its feelings?"

I laughed and shook my head.

"Shee-yit." The Mexican was laughing too. "I just rent one when I need to, man." A moment passed, then the Mexican leaned close to the window so his jowly face was an inch from the glass. "This thing even run?" he said, and I knew the hook was in.

"Like a fuckin' top!" Tommy said. "I'm telling you, it's brand new!" He opened the door beside me, folding my seat forward as if I wasn't in it as he reached for the chainsaw.

I just went for the ride. Let the time pass. Endured Tommy's bragging and addle-brained ranting and un-broken chain of off-the-cuff jokes that sometimes were so clever I wondered why the guy was such an imbecile. We wound up in a filthy house on a backroad, occupied by an obese papa, a fat, scraggly mama, and a gothic teenage daughter who looked at me either like she was interested or like she resented me for seeing how she lived.

Tommy jabbed his chin at me and said, "This is my cousin, Sam. Don't mind him, he fell down and hit his head a few dozen times," then laughed at his own joke, coaxing laughter out of everyone else. I got the impression Tommy had spent a lot of time with these people and that he made them nervous.

Silence settled over the room again and Tommy laughed at nothing and said, "Don't everyone talk at once," which elicited another ripple of nervous laughter. Then he said, "Craig, we got some special business for you. *Garage* business."

So we went through a kitchen of high stacks of dirty dishes, ancient appliances and peeling linoleum, and out a side door. Craig hit the switch and fluorescent lights stuttered to life and we filed into a garage with a tepid, dying smell to it, like a warm refrigerator. The place was piled with papers and rusty tools and a general, insane confusion of garbage from one end to the other. We followed the fat man as he picked a path through the junk, then watched as he keyed a padlock on the top door of an old metal locker of the kind that are racked up by the hundred in the hallways of high schools.

Inside were cardboard boxes, plastic bags, and a couple of loose weapons. "There it is," Tommy said. "How about some knucks?" He seemed a full foot taller than the fat man.

"How about *these* bad boys?" Craig was holding up

something that didn't resemble my idea of brass knuckles. They looked like a knife handle with a skull-head at the base and four loops of metal for fingers on the front. Without warning he tossed them to me and I jerked my hands up and caught them. I was immediately impressed by their weight. I put my fingers through the loops, closed my hand on the contoured handle, and there was a flutter in my stomach. If I'd hit Owen with *these* last night...

"Those are a felony to even *have*," Craig said, his black-bagged eyes weighing into me.

"Didn't I tell you? This is my cousin, man." All the humor was gone from Tommy's voice. "He's solid. He's good. Don't even sweat it."

"I ain't sweatin' it, I'm just saying. He might not know how shit works. I don't need anything coming back on me."

"Sam's good. You want those, Sam?"

"Yeah."

Tommy looked at Craig. "I got two bills. We need something else too. Something that *shoots*."

"Shit."

"Don't 'shit' me, brother. I'm talking a pea-shooter. No fuckin' Dirty Harry cannon. Come on, man. What do you think, I've joined the force?"

Craig looked from Tommy to me, his head beginning to nod. "Okay." He looked at me. "You ever shoot a gun?"

"No."

"Don't let this thing go off accidentally when you're figuring it out. And don't forget, you get caught with this motherfucker, you found it. You hear me? It was in the bushes by the sidewalk or something. I don't give a shit. You make up something and you stick to it no matter what. You mention me to the cops? I mean, your cousin here, him and me go way back, but..."

"I got it," I said.

"Didn't I tell you?" Tommy said, looking disgusted. "This is my cuz, man. Me and him are cut from the same cloth."

Craig responded with a pregnant glare, but just said, "Hang on. I got just the thing for you."

Tommy sang as he drove, jabbing his thumb at his chest: *"He's Mister Save-The-Fuckin'-Day when he wants to be! He's one heck of a guy, and I'm talkin' 'bout ...Me!"* He was proud of himself. I had asked and he had delivered as if he could magically produce money and weapons any day of the week. He had sold the chainsaw for nearly three hundred dollars, cleared a little cash for himself and armed me as well—all, he pointed out, before lunchtime. It was a rush, a morning of pure hustling, and only now did Tommy say, "So what the fuck you gonna do now that we got you armed?"

"I don't know," I said. "Nothing, maybe." I was holding the little revolver between my knees, carefully pointing it at the floor of my car, imagining thrusting it into Owen's face and saying, "What now, bitch?" I felt alternately dangerous and foolish. At moments I was outside myself, looking down, and it seemed I was a character in some alarmist film about lost kids turning to crime and dying in hails of bullets. The gun smelled like oil and I couldn't tell for sure, but it looked quite old. I had heard of it—a .38 Special—and recognized its snub-nosed shape from television and movies, but couldn't say much more about it—except it felt nice, substantial and menacing, in my hand.

We parked and bought hot dogs at Duane's Dogs on Beach Street. I bought. Tommy got three dogs and a large Coke and was still in the driver's seat as he ate. The sun beat on the windshield and it would have been a pleasant enough little lunch if it wasn't for the circumstances.

Tommy leaned in front of the rearview and cleaned mustard off his lips, checked his teeth, and said as he swallowed, "Come on, man, I thought my little cousin Sammy was a pacifist, so spill it, will you?" He gestured at the gun.

"Jill," I said. "She was raped."

He froze. His tongue was digging at food-mush and he stopped with the bulge in his cheek and rotated toward me.

"And I know who did it." My voice sounded strange.

"So you went off all heroic and pissed off and got your ass beat?"

"There were five guys there."

"Sammy, Sammy, Sammy." He took my knee in his meaty hand and shook my leg. "Why didn't you call me?

Who the fuck is it, some fucking Del Mar punks? We'll just catch your guy somewhere, Sam. They'll never find him. Fuck. You know where he lives? I'm serious here."

"Naw, he lives in this town. It's a guy I knew in school. Owen Ferguson—"

"*That* guy? Oh, man."

I felt a change in the air; a change in Tommy. I looked over. "You know him?"

"Shit, man. What's that song? You don't pull Superman's cape, you don't spit into the wind? You don't fuck around with Owen Ferguson."

"Yeah, well, I already did." I told Tommy how I'd spilled Owen's beer down his shirtfront and socked him, and how it had ended. Tommy shook his head over and over as I spoke, muttering *fuck*s and *shit*s.

"Listen," Tommy said. "Those dudes are serious. Owen Ferguson's got him a reputation. He thinks he's fuckin' Tony Soprano. I mean, what do you think you're gonna do?"

I looked at his forced expression of sincerity and concern and my horizons shifted again. I had been imagining Tommy as my ace in the hole, a sort of lowlife superhero I could summon in my hour of need, but I saw how foolish I had been. It should have dawned on me when he didn't even ask why I wanted a gun, for Christ's sake. He was too much what he was to help someone—even me—if he couldn't make out some shitty little profit margin for himself. I knew he would make promises and I would be waiting for him to show up and help me and

I'd be waiting forever. And the next time I saw him—if I was still alive to see him again—he would make jokes and act as if none of this had ever happened. And if I pressed it, if I confronted him, flat-out called him a liar, he would become indignant and find a reason to storm off.

"Forget it, Tommy," I said.

"Look, I mean, you can't just wave a fucking gun at Owen Ferguson and think you made your point, you know? You gotta be as bad as him, and that's pretty fuckin' bad."

"What about you?" My voice was rising. "You're 'pretty fuckin' bad,' aren't you? You're always saying it."

"It ain't just me, Sam! You're talking about starting a war. I could fuck your friend Owen up, okay? I could slap that kid around and make him fuckin' like it. But what? Do you think it's gonna end there? You tell me."

I could see his point. We stared at each other for a moment. He dragged his sleeve across his mouth.

"And it's all or nothing," he said. "Say I back you up, and say you give him a beating and then we get out of there. You think you're gonna be safe the next day? The next week? Ever fuckin' again? You might as well just walk up to him and shoot him in the face if you're gonna do anything at all."

A few seconds lapsed while I frowned and nodded. "Well, what would you do if you were me?" I said.

He started to say something, then stopped, thought it through and started again. "I don't know, Sam. I don't know. I guess if I was you I'd have to decide if I was willing to do some time over this shit. You got things pretty good. You're going to college."

"Fucking *junior* college," I said.

"Yeah? Well, then you transfer, right?"

"Yeah, sure." I wanted to end the discussion. "Listen," I said, "I'll figure out what I'm gonna do and just call you if I need anything else."

Tommy said, "Okay," and I could see those mad wheels spinning in his head. I knew he would keep his cell phone turned off for the next week or two.

I drove him back to his gas station. At every new landmark he asked me to turn here, it would only take a minute, he needed to stop at his friend's house, or a girl's house, or an enemy's house because they owed him money or had some drugs or a five-hundred-dollar motorcycle helmet or a pneumatic nail gun that he needed to pick up. I gave him a flat *no* each time. I explained to him that I had to get myself home.

I had to work tonight.

SEVEN

I had settled on a plan, or rather, a plan had percolated up from my subconscious. As I drove home to get cleaned up for work, I began entertaining a fantasy of Owen walking into Vanguard like he had two nights ago, attempting to intimidate me, to slap me around. I imagined myself just thrusting the gun into his face and clenching the trigger, bursting the back of his head out like the cap popping off a shaken up soda bottle, spraying blood and brain matter ten feet behind him before he slumped into a boneless pile on the maroon floor mat. I would claim self-defense. I would say he was trying to rob the store. I would say I found the pistol in the bushes outside and the cops would never be able to prove different. There might be a trial, I might get charged with some watered-down violent crime, but I would know for the rest of my life that I had executed the son of a bitch who had raped my girlfriend.

I wanted to be attacked, that was my entire plan; and, once attacked, I wanted to lash out with righteous and devastating force and kill Owen Ferguson. It amounted to a kind of jujitsu; it relieved me of the tension and responsibility of being the aggressor, allowed me to react rather than initiate.

And now I was armed for that reaction. I put on my old brown derby jacket that had been a favorite garment for too many years. It was separating at the seams, the pocket linings were shredded, the collar frayed. But I stood before a mirror wearing it, with the pistol in the right pocket and the knuckles in the left, and it made sense. The pockets had zippers so I could keep the weapons in place, and my hands were practiced at finding the tabs and slipping the zippers down. I went through a couple of practice draws and found the pistol slid free without snags and was in the open air, ready to kill in a few heartbeats—although it caught on the strips of torn lining and pulled the pocket inside out.

But nothing happened. The shift crawled by peacefully. Several times my heart began jumping as I thought I saw Owen's car rolling up, but it was always a cheap imitation. I called Jill at her mother's at eight o'clock and was told by her stepfather that she was out somewhere and she would call me back. She never called and it set my nerves on edge, left me agitated and reckless. I closed the store at ten, activated the alarm and let myself out. I locked the door and turned back toward my car in the empty parking lot, only then seeing the two of them advance.

They were both Mexican, wearing the gangland uniform, the combination cholo and black gangsta gear—both in baggy pants and baseball caps and oversized T-shirts. And they were coming on fast.

It was no good. I wanted Owen, but he sensed, maybe, how close to the edge I was. Or maybe he wanted to show me that I was light-work, that beating down a white punk like me was beneath him. Whatever had happened, he had elected to send these two thugs, probably paid them in coke or pot, maybe just said he'd consider it a favor if that one white boy who works at Vanguard got his ass beat.

I watched them strutting and rolling toward me in the dark parking lot, their arms wide, hands open, bodies loose and ready for action. I stood still until they were ten feet off and then I slid the zipper down, took out the heavy little revolver and extended it toward them.

They stopped mid-step. A car whisked by on the street beyond the shrubbery. A parking lot light rained down on the empty pavement behind them and turned them into silhouettes. One was anorexically thin, the other thick but strong, a weightlifter under a layer of fat with the proud posture and jerky energy of a gamecock.

The same light making the gangsters into silhouettes must have made my every detail visible to them. I was aware of my pocket lining hanging out, and a part of me wanted to put the gun in the other hand and stuff it back in so I didn't look like a jackass, but I thought they might jump at me in that moment. Instead, as I've seen done in so many movies, I cocked the pistol with my thumb. That ominous *click* had the expected, dramatic effect.

But I didn't feel like Clint Eastwood when I spoke. I could hear my voice quavering. "I'll just fuckin' shoot you guys and tell the cops everything that's happened. It'll be self-defense. If you want to die I don't give a fuck."

I heard the skinny one breathe, *"Fu-u-uck!"* but the gamecock shook his head sadly and said, "Damn, Homes. You just fucked up bad. You was just gonna get beat down. Now you're dead, aye."

I moved the gun a little. "Not tonight I'm not."

They had a quick exchange in Spanish and then the gamecock pointed at me. "You just made it a thousand times worse for yourself, white bread."

When the Mexican kids used to call me "white bread" in school, I always answered by calling them "toast." It crossed my mind but cute comebacks seemed asinine just now. I just kept the gun extended and waited.

The stout gangster finally hit the skinny one on the shoulder and started turning away.

I kept the gun extended.

"Later, bitch," the gamecock said, and I almost shot him in the back as he strutted off. I kept the gun trained on them as they rounded the building out of sight, but as much as I wanted to show Owen how afraid he ought to be, I couldn't just squeeze that trigger. I was nothing but relieved as the two thugs disappeared from my view.

I kept the gun in my hand as I started my car, and kept it beside me as I drove home. I slept on the couch with the gun on the coffee table, after making a madman's door chime out of a pan and some silverware tied together with a shoelace and hung on the doorknob. If anyone tried to open the door the racket would wake me up and as soon as their head leaned in I'd squeeze off a round and their skull would flatten to a blanket of dark blood on the wall.

Or so I fantasized. Nobody came to the door. The night passed in shallow and fitful sleep and I found myself awake at dawn, staring at the ceiling. I lay there for an hour, until my cell phone, next to my keys on the coffee table, began ringing.

"Hi, Sam," Jill said. Her voice was a little gravelly. So was mine. It was ten after seven.

"Hey, are you okay? Have you...talked to anyone? You still at your mom's?"

There were two seconds of silence. "Yeah, I'm at my mom's. I went to the police. I had to go to Blackmer for that. And I was examined by a doctor."

"Yeah?"

"I'm still pregnant. Everything's normal."

I couldn't think of anything to say. I had, in truth, shoved this out of my mind. It was just too much for me to factor in. It wasn't real. How could we have a kid?

How could we pretend like it was a good idea when this black cloud had settled over our lives?

"Sam?"

"Yeah. I'm here."

"Aren't you relieved about that?"

"Yeah," I said. "Yes! Of course I am!"

I could hear her sniffling tears back. "What happened doesn't change *anything* for me. It shouldn't change anything for you either!"

"Jill!" I said. "It doesn't. Listen, everything's going to be fine, okay? I just need to get my head straight a little. Are you okay otherwise?"

"I'm perfectly fine."

I told her she just needed to sit tight and get better and I'd find us a new place real soon. I told her I was coming to see her in an hour or two, but she said to wait. It was my night off and she suggested we see a movie, have dinner and try to be normal. She needed it right now, she said. I agreed even as I scoffed to myself. *Try to be normal?* I thought. My heart was thudding, slowly and heavily, as if it resented the effort. My mind was repeating Owen Ferguson's name like a primitive war chant and sweat had broken out at my hairline. Me having a kid. And the mother of my child raped. And me knowing who did it and trying to be *normal*.

When she hung up I tossed the cell onto the coffee table, picked up my gun, rose and headed toward the shower. I had shined off my classes yesterday, but my conscience nagged. I had paid the money; I had bragged that I would make something of myself. Jill didn't want to see me this morning anyway and I was going to start upending tables and smashing windows if I just sat here. What the hell.

Blackmer's extension of Morse Junior College in Del Mar was held in what had once been the city post office—an old building that would shudder and crumble and crush us all to death if there happened to be an earthquake of any magnitude. No big loss. I sat in the back, my pummeled face clean shaven, my hair combed, and nobody spent too much time looking at me. I was at a desk that might have been manufactured in 1962, staring at Ms. Hatley-Lester—the self-assured, crew-cut, flat-chested instructor—as she droned on in a masculine monotone about how our whole reality was manufactured by the "controlled mass media." The class was called Twenty-First Century Social Problems with a textbook of the same name that I had paid thirty bucks for, and its aim was to let me know that, by the way, pal, you're a slave. There is no government, there's nobody looking out for you, there's just a bunch of demonic power players pulling strings, consolidating power, butchering children. Sometimes she showed us documentaries that were at once so convincing and logical, and so opposed to everything I thought I knew, that I came away feeling like my own name might be a lie.

Today, after the introductory monologue, the room was darkened and an old video tape, that must have been shown to dozens of classes to date, was popped into a VCR that lived on a wheeled metal stand with "MJC" stencilled onto it. The subject of the movie was going to be the invasion of Panama in the '80s and the disparity between what had actually happened and what our filthy, sick-minded, hell-spawned excuse for a government and its lapdog media told us had happened.

The movie got underway. There was a silhouette of a woman and the quiet sound of her speaking whatever language they speak in Panama, and then the translator's voice overlapping at full volume, "The shooting began at midnight..."

I couldn't sit still. I didn't disbelieve the documentary and I wasn't offended by it, I just didn't give a shit. I was thinking about having a kid in a few short months. I was thinking of walking around with Jill when her stomach grew round and heavy, and then walking with a stroller in front of us, and then me acting out the role of father for the next two decades and always looking at my family and remembering, *knowing*.

I had something growing in me too, expanding in my chest and in my braincase so I had to shut my eyes tight and try to catch my breath. But it wouldn't stop. It was taking on a more distinct shape, moment by moment, and now it was starting to kick.

I grabbed up my book and notepad and stood. I didn't look around, just floated toward the door and then I was in the bright hallway, moving toward the exit. I patted my pocket, not my right but my left, and squeezed my hand around the knuckles through the material of my jacket.

Somewhere along the way, living in this town most of my life, I acquired the knowledge of where Owen Ferguson's family lived. It was an old Victorian from Blackmer's heyday, now decaying in a decaying neighborhood on Third Street. I had passed the place a thousand times over the years and I always thought of Owen when I did. Six or eight years ago, when Owen himself had lived here, I used to see him coming or going, maybe leaning up against his lowered car outside, his body pressed against that of a girl with brown skin and hair frozen stiff and tall by Aqua Net. Very occasionally, Owen and I had made eye contact and once he even acknowledged me with an upward jerk of his eyebrows and a quiet, "What's up."

I had seen his mother from time to time too. A rough-hewn, middle aged white lady, thick at the waistline with deflated cleavage and raunchy clothes. She had a craggy face and frazzled yellow hair with dark roots. Owen's biological father was a mystery and his stepfather long gone to prison, but he had a half brother, Ramón, and, as I was to learn, a six-year-old half sister.

Ramón's story was the inverse of Owen's. A half-Mexican who didn't take part in the local gangs, knew only a few scraps of Spanish, and spent as little time as possible in the poor and dangerous neighborhoods. Ramón had crossed over to smoke pot and party with the white skateboarders, punks and heavy metal kids and when he spoke his English, rather than being accented like a second language, was pure California stoner.

I had seen Ramón at dozens of parties since high school and had watched as he coerced girls into leaving with him or discussed in a shouting, garrulous voice what girls he'd like to try at and how tormented he was by whose tits and ass. He made me think of a repulsively spoiled four-year-old, used to getting what he wanted through the tactic of making noise and asking for it over and over until he was appeased. And the astounding thing was that it worked so often.

I can call half a dozen occasions to mind when Ramón successfully attached himself to a girl that I lacked the nerve to even say hello to. I have the somehow disturbing memory of Ramón dragging a former cheerleader named Ashley Thorne through a cluster of cars parked outside a keg party. It was dark—after midnight—and a group of us stared as the girl laughed and allowed the little man to pull a door open on a tan Scout and to shove her in. I had been fascinated by Ashley Thorne through my teenage years and had had a crush on her, like most of the young men at Blackmer High, but that night I had shouted and laughed as she was destroyed for me, as the car began rocking and that princess was made use of like a glaze-eyed teenage junkie. And we all laughed harder later, when Ramón told us he didn't even know whose car it had been.

I guess Ramón appealed to girls the way children do. His face was round, small on his head like a baby's, and he had rather large and bright green eyes that I can't recall ever seeing other than bloodshot. His hair was black and seemed to grow like an animal's pelt, close and short and straight back from his hairline.

It had probably been more than a year since I had last thought of Ramón, and I may not have ever thought of him again if I hadn't seen him park a junky little Ford in front of his mother's house as I staked the place out. I watched him stand up and slam the door. His arrogance was obvious even as he stood out of that eight-hundred-dollar car in front of that seedy and decomposing Victorian. He was wearing shades and carrying a plastic grocery bag and I noticed then something I had never noticed before—how brown his skin is.

And all at once I was wildly and irrepressibly certain that he had been the Hispanic party—the brown-skinned piece of filth—who had helped Owen rape Jill. This was infinitely possible, I told myself, since Ramón existed on the fringes of the gang world and he logically had a stake in his brother's battles. And he was such a crass, relentless little womanizer that he lived his whole life a mere nudge from simply pinning down and raping the girls he had set his sights on.

Or maybe I didn't suspect him for even an instant. Maybe Ramón had just presented his despicable self like a clay pigeon at the very moment that I was looking for something to take a potshot at. Maybe if I was being perfectly frank with myself I would have admitted that I was looking for a raw nerve to torture. I was fraying at the edges from lack of real sleep and every minor irritation was sending me into a spiral of violent impulses. Maybe if I had seen Owen's mother first I would have found a way to rationalize skulking up behind her and kicking her in the center of the back, sending her sprawling on the sidewalk and then spitting on her, cursing her for coupling with lowlifes and spawning a rapist like Owen Ferguson.

I stood out of my car and felt the sunlight on my back and the heat rising off the street. I took off my shades and threw them on the seat and gently closed the driver's door. The sky was a clear, blinding blue and plants and lawns were deep green. The springtime weather made even this street pretty. There was a murmur of activity in the neighborhood, kids shouting, cars giving prolonged exhales as they passed, but nobody noticed me.

I felt strange. Not afraid anymore, but high. Exhilarated. Almost in a dream state. I now could see what made these thugs tick, how they did the unthinkable without a moment of hesitation, and how it could become addictive. I wiggled my fingers in the metal holes and closed my fist on the knife-handle grip of the brass knuckles. I lifted my eyes to Ramón's back as he ascended the tall, sun-bleached staircase of the chipped Victorian, and I started after him.

He was just pushing the heavy, wide front door open when he became aware of my footsteps clomping up behind him and deigned to turn around. He managed to look bored as he faced me, and if, when I raised my fist, his eyes widened behind his black sunglasses, I'll never know.

I hurled the knuckles into his cheek, harder than I had planned, and his face seemed to pucker around the point of impact. Blood was already gooping from his skin as he toppled. He turned a little and landed on top of his plastic grocery bag halfway into the relatively dark room, where I could now hear a TV going.

He was starting to rise and I kicked him viciously in the seat of his factory-faded jeans, scooting him forward a foot. My voice came out as a growl. "Did you rape her, you fucking piece of shit?!?" One part of my mind stood in judgment, observing quietly, telling me I was unhinged and I had better be careful. I tried to listen to it, even as I leered like a madman and my muscles twitched with the impulse to kill a wounded thing.

I bent, blinking as my eyes adjusted to the light inside the house, and I took Ramón's shirt collar in my left hand. I had the knuckles elevated and I felt like I could collapse his skull with one punch. As my pupils dilated I saw that Ramón's cheek was torn wide open and the blood was coursing steadily with his pounding heart, washing down his face like water over a rock in a creek. His shades were off and his green eyes were fixed on me with an expression of utter stupidity, like a run-over dog flopped onto the hot roadside, taking its last rapid breaths with its intestines glistening in front of it.

"Answer me you little punk! Cocksucker! Answer me!

You go to my apartment a couple nights ago? Huh? You and Owen?"

I became aware of whimpering and glanced up at a little Mexican girl staring at me from the couch. She was wearing a white nightgown and had bright green eyes. She had been watching Jerry Springer and the man's smug, asinine fucking repartee and his perverted good humor made me want to projectile vomit.

"Dude!" Ramón finally said from the floor, his eyes alive again, dazzled by recognition. "Sam! Hey! Schuler! What the fuck, Sam?" He squirmed but made no real effort to get his shirtfront free of my grip.

And then the mother came in and raised a scream that made me want to leap over Ramón and knock her cold. "WHAT'S GOING ON! OH MY GOD! WHAT IS THIS?" She was worse than the picture of her I carried in my head, because she had obviously been asleep in some musty corner of the house. She wore no pants, just a huge purple T-shirt with some grotesque sparkled design on it. Her legs were skinny, paper white and bruised and the contrast with her puffy upper body made me think of Tweedle Dum. "OH MY GOD! STOP IT, PLEASE!" she bellowed. Her hair looked like moldy straw; it was lopsided, mashed upward on one side from her pillow. There was mascara smeared around eyes the same shape and shade of blue as Owen's.

"Lady!" I said, still crouching, still poised to bang the knuckles into Ramón's face. "Shut the fuck up! You know what kind of fucking scum you've got living with you? Huh?"

The little girl goggled at me. She had suctioned herself against her mother's side.

"Oh my gaaaaawd!" the woman squeaked this time, at a low volume, sounding as if she had just learned of a dear one's death. She was staring at the massive amount of blood now pooling on the worn hardwood beneath Ramón's head. The blood was pink at the edge of the puddle, mixing with white and I grunted. A half gallon of milk had been in the grocery bag and had split open when Ramón fell on it. His mother looked as if she thought the white was somehow leaking from her son, indicating some unnatural, doubtlessly fatal injury. She raised both her hands to me and simpered, "I don't know what happened, okay? But let him up, okay? We can talk about this!"

I released Ramón's shirtfront and straightened, lifting the brass knuckles, brandishing them in front of me. "I'll tell you what happened, lady. Someone raped my girl-friend. *Owen*—your son—raped her—"

"No—"

"SHUT THE FUCK UP! Yes, he did. And maybe this little faggot was in on it! And if he was I'm gonna fuckin' KILL him!"

"Sam!"

I looked down at Ramón, now propped on an elbow in his blood and milk. He had his hand flattened over the gashed side of his face, covering one eye. The other eye was wide, the iris blazing at me, floating in the white like a greened penny.

"Listen, dude, you're fucking up." The eye blinked. He sounded calm. Confident. "I'm telling you the truth, bro. I don't know what happened with Owen. I don't know if he did what you say. All I know is I wasn't there. I swear to God. But listen, you know Owen. You shouldn't have pulled this fucking shit. You're dead now."

I lifted my right foot from behind Ramón and took a step backward. "*Fuck* Owen," I said, and punched the wall next do the doorjamb for emphasis. The brass knuckles dented the plaster, but I cut my own knuckles open in the process and it ratcheted up my anger again. "You just wait and see what happens to Owen." I shook the knuckles, my index finger peeled off and pointing. I looked down. "And you better hope I never learn you had anything to do with it, Ramón, you little bitch!"

The mother was staring at me, stroking her daughter's hair, panting like she'd just stopped jogging. But she didn't say a word. She didn't want to interrupt my withdrawal from her house.

"I'm sorry about scaring the little girl," I said.

I departed with the door standing open behind me, dropped down the steps and crossed the sunny street in the indifferent neighborhood, sliding the brass knuckles off my hand.

I went back home to sit and watch the door. To wait for Owen to come, as he surely would.

But he never showed up.

EIGHT

I started getting ready at four-thirty and picked Jill up
from her mother's at six. As soon as she saw me she broke
down, touching my battered face, unable to speak for her
weeping. I found myself becoming sheepish, putting on
an act, and then found myself lying very smoothly. I was
upset so I got drunk and got stupid, I said. Mouthed off
to a bunch of guys in a bar and got stomped on a little. It
was nothing, nothing. Let's try to enjoy ourselves
tonight, I said. She didn't have the emotional resources
just now to explore the possibility that what I said wasn't
true and she finally nodded, took my arm, and we left.

The restaurant was called Maurice's; a dim, deter-
minedly classy French place. I have an aversion to these
restaurants. I feel like the mark in a con operation, as if
the servers and cooks will be in the back after closing,

laughing and slapping each other on the back, eating hamburgers and talking about the fools they lured in and neatly extracted money from. There is something vaguely humiliating about it. The food always seems to answer to a taste I have yet to acquire, the candlelight and gaudy music lay the atmosphere on a little too thick to be believable, the waiters seem to be on the verge of smirking, covering their faces and chuckling, at which point the whole facade would go up in vapor and I would stand, snarling, and ask them what the hell they were trying to pull. But the facade never cracks. You are lured in, seated, talked down to, and not until the bill is delivered do you realize how thoroughly you've been had.

Tonight, however, I shut up and played along. The waiter was a slim, middle-aged gay man, and I didn't comment on it. The portions were small and strange, and I ate all the bread in the basket and dabbed the butter from my mouth with the cloth napkin and said how good everything was.

It wasn't, in truth, all that difficult with Jill across from me. She had made a job of dressing for the evening, with that pride and resourcefulness that certain girls take in their appearance, and it made me feel like we were on a first date two years ago. Men's eyes lingered on her as we entered the restaurant and our waiter seemed pleased with her, wishing, I guess, that he could look just like that. Her shirt was snug and scooped low at the neck and her skin glowed. Her makeup was subtle, applied cleverly so a face I had looked at a million times became a brand new distraction.

With my bruised face and general lack of style, I felt like a panhandler she was treating to a meal. I took off my old brown derby jacket, hoping my button-down shirt would be somewhat more appropriate. When I hung the jacket on the back of my chair, it hung oddly and the weapons clumped against the chair legs.

Jill smirked at me. "You got rocks in your pockets?"

"I'm just happy to see you," I said, then tried again: "Yeah, rocks. You know, in case the waiter takes too long, I can nail him—"

"He'd probably like that," she said, and I laughed. The good humor was slightly forced, but better than the alternative. But her eyes held me and the juice went out of her smile. "So what's in your pockets?"

"Nothing." I shook my head. "Don't worry about it."

"Okay, then. What happened to your knuckles?"

I looked down. Two of my knuckles were scraped, the middle one bruised as well. I sighed. My mind raced ahead and I knew I couldn't bring reality crashing down on us right now.

"The cash register at work," I said. "You know the little springs on the little metal things that hold the money down? Well you reach in there at the end of the night to get all the bills out, and the end of the spring goes right under your fingernail. Never fails. It gets a nerve under there, hurts all the way up to your shoulder."

She was looking at me a little too hard, trying, it

seemed, to see around my lie.

"So," I said. "When it happened last night I got pissed and punched the edge of the counter."

"Sam! You need to control your temper."

"I know."

"And I'm not even going to ask you what's in your jacket pockets." Her eyes glittered. "I've forgotten all about it."

Our eyes remained locked for several seconds and that look had more meaning than any of the conversation. That look said that we were both here pretending and it was okay.

It was a relief, that moment of speaking with our eyes. I had been worrying on some level that she was damaged so profoundly she would never quite touch down on the real world again.

The movie was an idiotic hottest-new-slapstick by a team that had made one genuinely funny movie a few years ago the way a drunken, blindfolded man with a pistol might nail the bull's eye on a shooting range. Now they were squeezing off random shots in every direction, not even sure, evidently, where the target was anymore. The movie afforded us possibly two real laughs in two hours, for twenty dollars. Afterward we drove out to the cliffs overhanging the Pacific and parked and had sex in the backseat of my Fairlane to the static-crashing of waves. Jill was lively and horny, determined that our sex be good, and she managed to banish all ghosts of her rape from the inside of the car. The windows fogged over and after a while she pushed me down so I lay on my back and then climbed on and grounded me deep into her until she reached orgasm. Then she lay down and pulled me over her and I began that last sprint to the top of the mountain, where you finally run up and jump off and freefall for a moment and then land back in your skin again, gasping. She let me come inside her because she was pregnant anyway and she clung to me as I did, groaning with me and stroking the back of my head while I convulsed against her damp, lithe body.

I left her at her mother's at two in the morning, and she told me that whatever I was doing with whatever was in my pockets I had better be careful. I had better remember how much she needed me.

I had turned off my cell phone in the movie theater and didn't turn it back on until I was driving home. There was one message from a number I had never seen before. No name. I dialed in and played the message and the Brando voice said, "You're dead, motherfucker," followed by a click.

My heart exploded to a gallop. The terror was back and shutting down my body. The black freeway slipped by outside and I flew along in hurtling and surreal motion but if I had been standing on my own two feet I would have been groping for support. My evening with Jill, getting out of Blackmer, had made the lunatic violence of the morning like something I had dreamed. Our normalcy, our sex, had made the rape feel insignificant. A mere speed bump, already behind us and forgotten. But that was a fiction. It was a spell cast by Jill's cleverness and female instincts. I was crossing back over now as if my car was passing through some force field that surrounded Blackmer, and fear began burning in my stomach as I reentered the world of dirt and gangsters where I felt the need to weigh myself down with brass knuckles and the mean little revolver.

My mind was leaping ahead, and I had the foresight to leave my car across the street from my building in the parking lot of a darkened shopping center. I crossed Murdock Avenue, went down the walkway, and crept up the cement steps with my back to the wall. I felt like a fool, imitating the hundred thousand cops & robbers programs I'd seen, but I took the .38 from my pocket and cocked it, held it up next to my shoulder, at the ready, just like my TV had taught me.

There was no sign of anyone as I reached the landing. I thought ahead once more and saw myself maybe finally sleeping. I would put the door chime in place again and there would be no way anyone could get the drop on me so tonight, finally, I would relax.

I passed the gun to my left hand and fished out my keys. I slid the correct one into the slot and turned it, but felt looseness, realizing with disgust that I had left the thing unlocked. But would I do something that stupid? I frowned, feeling amused, even, as I tried to remember if I had remembered to rock the knob, to check that the lock was set when I left this evening. But the black dizzying horror rose up behind my eyes. I heard or felt or sensed the presence on the other side of that dense door—as if, I thought, my key snicking in the slot had stirred someone to action. A noise reached my ears—a male voice—*"He's here! He's here!"*—and I was already flinging myself away.

Later I would berate myself in the vilest language. Where had all my fantasies of heroics gone? Wasn't this my chance? I stumbled once on the steps, caught myself on the iron railing in mid-tumble and kicked my legs out before me and kept moving. I hit the walkway and could hear them coming now, their shoes slapping the cement stairs as I darted ahead and all but dove between another set of buildings and down another walkway.

A half dozen of the ground level apartments have miniature back yards enclosed by five foot wooden walls and I dove over the first wall, hardly touching it in my adrenaline high. I landed like a cat and flattened myself to the damp grass. Beside me there was a tarp draped over some bicycles and I inched underneath it, cringing at its deafening crinkling but pulling its corner down until I was halfway hidden. I kept the gun raised, hugging myself against the cool bike frames and releasing my breath in shuddering gasps.

A half hour passed. The gun was still in my hand, although I had uncocked it. Nobody had come by this yard, nobody had looked for me here. My joints were stiff from curling my frame into a ball. My knees ached as my legs unfolded. I dropped the gun into my pocket and boosted myself over the wall. I circled out of the apartment complex, walked two blocks out of the way and entered the dark shopping center from the far end. My car sat by itself, a pale vessel anchored in a black asphalt sea. I had a moment of panic in which I slapped my front pockets, reached in and found my keys still there, and then I broke into a run, made it to my car, and drove off toward the only place I could think of.

NINE

My grandfather's pickup and my grandmother's clean, neat lower-middleclass Ford Taurus were in the driveway. The neighborhood slept, utterly. I rolled past the house and pulled to the end of the street, rounded the corner, and parked in the alleyway, edging to my right until the side mirror touched the outside of the backyard fence my grandfather had built twenty years before. It was nearly four a.m. I could feel the fingers of exhaustion clawing at my mind, trying to get a good grip and pull it down into the quicksand of unconsciousness.

I walked around the front, found the door locked, and, having no other choice, knocked.

Within moments I was facing my grandfather in his robe. He was shrunken, stooped with age and gray, although there were still proud streaks of dark in his hair.

His face was a collapsed, creased thing, the skin drooping as if melting, and his eyes had a wet sparkle in the half-light. The doctor had recently told him his heart might stop at any moment but he stood before me like a dangerous man, unblurred from sleep, because, I knew, he didn't sleep at night.

"Jesus-God, Sam!" he said. "I almost knocked your goddamned head off. What the hell are you doing?"

I saw he had a nine-iron in his right hand as I passed inside.

"Well?" he said. He hadn't spoken in hours, was probably sitting in front of his computer when I knocked, and his voice was a growl. "Jesus! What the hell happened to your face, Sam?"

"Sorry about this, Grandpa. It's a long, long story. Listen, can I tell it to you tomorrow and sleep on the couch tonight?"

He looked at me for a moment, shook his head and smiled. "Christ. Be my guest." I could almost read his thoughts. He was imagining I had gone drinking, got in some fistfight and my girlfriend had kicked me out for the night. "There are some blankets in the hall closet, I think. We'll talk about this in the morning."

And then he walked off. A moment later I heard him talking to my grandmother as he ushered her back into their bedroom. "It's nothing," he said. "It's just Sam. Yes, Sam. He had a fight with his girlfriend or something and is going to sleep on the couch." And then he went into the bedroom across the hall, where he surfed the web and talked to other ancient, insomniac Republicans all night, and the door latch clicked.

I found a heavy knit blanket, stripped to my underwear and fell onto the couch, passing through the cushions and tumbling down, down, down with the ether of dreams closing around me.

In the morning I found myself flaunting my horrendous circumstances before Grandpa Art and Grandma Anne while not wanting to say the first word about the last few days. Especially to my grandmother.

My grandparents raised me here in Blackmer and they were, for practical purposes, my parents. But as the years had gone forward they had become Old People. My grandmother, especially, had settled into the role of an Old Lady and the chasm between what she saw and what was actually before her seemed to widen each day. Nothing could compel me to lift up the damp rock of my calm demeanor and show her the things crawling inside my mind. But, by a reverse equation, I imagined explaining all this to my grandfather like a man in a confession booth, and getting a no-bullshit, old-world solution handed to me in a couple of quick phrases.

I ate the eggs and toast my grandmother made me, gulped the strong coffee they lived off of, and told her it was nothing. I even made my pummeled face into a smile. I told her just what she and my grandfather had assumed: I had gone out drinking and got into a fight, and Jill had gotten upset and locked me out of the apartment. Ha-ha. Jill and I will come over in a month or two, we'll all have dinner together and laugh about it.

I was sopping up the juice of the egg yolk with my toast, my grandmother clicking her tongue and shaking her head, when Grandpa Art's voice drove a cold spike into my chest.

"SAMUEL!" he said. "COME HERE, NOW!"

My grandmother looked at me from her post at the sink with something like horror, and I must have had the same expression. That guttural drill sergeant's bark had always, in my youth, been the harbinger of physical punishment. It was a sound of rage desperate for an outlet. I rose, feeling eleven years old, a foot shorter, and stepped into the living room and winced when I saw him there.

Grandpa Art was standing beside the coat rack that was behind the front door. The rack was heaped with his and my grandmother's jackets and coats, and he had my brown derby jacket in his hand. His gaze pushed at me like a hundred-mile-an-hour wind. The weapons in my jacket pockets stretched the material downward in an obvious fashion. I said, "Shit."

I had left the garment on the floor next to the couch, stuffed halfway under the end-table when I went to sleep, and then had awakened to my grandmother's call for breakfast and hadn't picked the thing up. So Grandpa Art had grabbed it off the floor to put it on the coat rack, felt the unusual weight and then explored inside the pockets.

Something shifted behind the old man's eyes as he

looked at the bruises and scuffs on my face. He seemed to realize the significance of everything—its cumulative effect. When he spoke, the rage had been replaced by quiet insistence, and he said, "We better have a talk, son."

I nodded.

I followed him to what he called his "lion's den," which was the garage off the side of the house. He had a miniature refrigerator out there, a TV, a space heater, and every power tool known to man, all organized as if by a secretary.

He walked out the front door ahead of me, carrying my jacket like an exhibit at a murder trial. It was another bright and cloudless morning. He lifted a hand and said hello to an old man in a duck hunting cap who was walking a small white dog up the sidewalk, and I remembered that these homes had all been staked out by retirees over the last decade. The popular local term for the neighborhood was the Limber Dick Community. I wondered what would happen when death thinned out the population, then looked at my grandfather's back and realized how soon I would have at least part of my answer. He was shrinking. Further gone each time I visited. His muscles vanishing, his old clothes, accustomed to the beef and strength of a workingman's build, drooping.

Grandpa Art had driven diesel rigs for thirty years and he adhered to the classic trucker dress code: the short-sleeved western shirt tucked into battered Levis, the work boots on the bottom and gray hair pomaded into a neat little almost-pompadour on top. His face always seemed carefully shaven, except for the thick sideburns that went down past his ever-growing ears. It was the uniform of a time and place, of a nearly extinct species— the belligerent middle-American redneck who had fought in Korea, come back with his faith unshaken, and then watched the 1960s unfold the way he might watch his house burn down. There had never been any Summer of Love for Arthur Schuler. He had no interest in Civil Rights, hippies or liberals—or Democrats for that matter. I heard him say once that it might have worked out very well if we had indeed brought all the planes back from Vietnam, just in time to napalm the Woodstock festival.

But the man had *lived*. He had been an orphan of the Great Depression and seen the country and the world. He had made his way, been a barroom fighter and—he hinted—a womanizer at some distant point in the twentieth century, and had come away with an instinct for life, for the things that people do and their base and predictable motivations.

We entered through the garage's side door. It was cool out here and had the somehow lifeless and businesslike atmosphere of a shed. My grandfather laid my jacket on the top of his workbench, the weapons giving muted thunks as they hit the metal top. He crouched and grunted and the antique garage door scraped in its tracks and slid up over our heads and the spring air and morning sunshine rushed in.

He indicated the swivel stool in front of the workbench and said, "Sit," and turned to his little refrigerator. He took out a beer and handed it off to me, cracked one for himself, took a long gulp and then stared down at me.

"Now tell me," he said.

And I did. I began with Rich stealing the pot and filled in every detail up to me running for my life last night. He shook his head the entire time, muttering things like "god-almighty!" and "Jesus-H-fucking-Christ!" and "Tommy? Aw, Sam, no!"

When I finished the story my grandfather was quiet for a long time. He had seated himself across from me, on a stack of ninety-pound bags of concrete mix, and a flush had come to his cheeks. He upended his beer and got another. I had seen this same attitude of distraction dozens of times, whenever he began to visualize a building project.

"Shit!" he kept sputtering. Then he looked up. "I ever tell you about Tommy's father? He was a tennis teacher, always worried about his hair, always trying to show off his muscles, making a comment to every girl that went by like a goddamn nigger on a street corner. He knocked up your Aunt Carrie and left town as fast as he could." Granpa Art winked. "But not before I made him hurt a little." He paused, let that soak, cleared his throat. "Point is, Tom Senior was a sneaky, lying, two-faced son of a bitch, and Tommy ain't any different. I don't care what anyone says, it's all genetics. I know it firsthand. He lived with me for a few years and I tried and tried to make a man of him, but it was no use. He wouldn't go to school.

Couldn't stay out of fights. Was already chasing girls nonstop when he was thirteen. He's just like his old man and there's nothing to be done about it."

I had forgotten how Grandpa Art was given to rambling these last couple of years. He could talk for fifteen minutes and not even approach the point he'd started off toward. He would just abandon the subject at hand, notice an interesting side-trail of memory and start down it without any logical segue. He sighed now, lost down one of these trails, and I just watched him, examining the elephant-hide cracks and wrinkles covering his face like a disease, the great stretched bags of flesh making his eyes look grave and sad.

"Anyway," he continued. "The point is that Tommy is just what he is. He's no good. But that night, shit, what was it? Nineteen-sixty-three? Sixty-four? Jesus, Sam, I'm *old*!" And he almost began a discussion of his age, but I saw him catch himself. "What was I saying? Oh yeah, that night I needed *four* buddies!" He folded his thumb against his palm and held up four thick fingers as if I might not catch on. "It took five of us to take on Tommy's old man, and even then we had one hell of a time knocking that son of a bitch down." He nodded and stared off, then returned. "So you see what I'm getting at."

"Tommy's dad was tough?" I said.

"What I'm saying is, Tommy does have his uses. He's got some natural gifts. His father was gifted—that guy could have played tennis professionally—but he was no good. *Undisciplined* was what he was. You see, what's happened here is you *can't* go to the police."

I rubbed the back of my neck and filled my lungs.

Grandpa Art thought a moment and said, "You know what a blood feud is?"

"A blood feud?"

"That's right. Like the Hatfields and McCoys. These Mexican gang kids live their lives looking for a blood feud, and you just handed 'em one! You went to this Owen character's house, for Christ's sake. Sam, you've bitched this thing up about as bad as you could. And there's no evidence of anything. That's what I was saying. You go to the police now and they might talk to this boy and tell him to leave you alone, but he can just send someone else, or he can wait and catch you next month. He's trying to be the toughest kid in town and he's gotta save face here. The only way you can get out of it now is to leave town.

"So that's why you gotta get hold of Tommy," he said. "Tommy's a no-good sonofabitch, but he's not stupid by any stretch. He's a resourceful shit, actually. He can do things when he sets his mind to it, it's just that all he ever sets his mind to is doing nothing. And I was saying how tough his father was? Well, Tommy is twice as tough. Men been in prison, they can't afford to stand around and *talk* about fighting. They take you apart as soon as look at you." He frowned. "You're out of your depth here, Sam. It's like they say, swimming with sharks. But Tommy…there's only one thing makes sense. So get on your little phone there and call him up."

"He's not going to answer," I said. "I already asked him for help and he just wiggled out of it."

"'Course he did. I could have told you he woulda done that. Just call him, will you? Let Grandpa Art talk to him."

I picked up my jacket, found the inner pocket and retrieved my cell. I opened it, punched through until I found Tommy's number and punched CALL. I waited a long time in the silent garage, listening to the mechanical rings, feeling my grandfather's stare, and just as I was about to give up I heard, "This is Tom."

"Tommy!" I said.

"I'm not by the phone but if you leave a message at the tone I'll get back to you as soon as possible." I almost laughed at his staid and stiff impersonation of a normal citizen.

"It's his answering machine," I said to Grandpa Art, knowing he would instantly understand "answering machine," but would scowl at me if I tried to explain it was the message service on his cell phone.

"Gimme that thing!" the old man snapped. "Tom?" he bellowed, standing up, pressing the device to his ear. "What the fuck are you doing to Sam, shithead? Where are you? You better call me back, you hear me? You're gonna get Sam out of this, or so help me Jesus I'm gonna see that your ass goes back to prison, and whoever your fat friend is with the guns and knives is gonna hear from the police too!" He winked at me. "You call me back the minute you get this message, you hear? I'm giving you until one o'clock. ONE O'CLOCK! And then I'm calling the cops, and you know goddamned well I will!" He gave his number and said, "You better step up to the plate, Tom!"

He tossed me the phone and I caught it and closed it, terminating the call.

Grandpa Art seemed to deflate and he sat down again on the cement bags. The line of light fell across his lower half, washing his withered denim knees in sunshine. His bottom lip sagged from his teeth. He sighed and looked up at me and the moment took on a portentous air. "I'll just say this, Sam: If it comes down to you or Tommy getting hurt, let it be him. I love him but he's no good to anyone. You, you've got a kid on the way, for Christ's sake. So don't get proud and do anything stupid. Anything *else* stupid, I mean. The regret you feel when you save your own skin, that lasts about five seconds, lemme tell you." He was looking out the garage opening, at the grill of his pickup. He leaned forward, stood with effort and placed a hand on my shoulder. "I gotta go lay down."

He began shuffling away and I felt a chill, thinking that, if such a thing was possible, I was feeling someone walk over his grave.

TEN

I retrieved my car from the alleyway, drove back into town, and parked once again in the lot of the shopping center across the street from my apartments. The shopping center was now alive if not quite busy. I locked my car and started home under the sunshine, seeing myself through the eyes of malignant onlookers I was only imagining. I went up the main walkway of the apartment facility and then up the cement stairs of my building, my hand on the gun in my pocket. I pulled the gun out and cocked it as I reached the landing.

The door was ajar and I pushed, took a breath and went in with the gun extended. I flashed it to my right but the living room was empty. There was no sign that anyone but me had been here. The blanket I had slept under the previous two nights was crumpled on the couch from yesterday morning. I flashed the gun to my left and followed it into the little five-foot hallway that opened to the bedroom and the bathroom. I jabbed the gun into each room, but I already knew I would find nothing. Sweat oozed in my armpits, my heart was pumping away like a steam engine. I let the gun sag. I wondered if they had worn gloves even, had guns with silencers so they could just execute me and disappear and deny everything. I wondered if I had imagined last night, but no—the door was ajar. It had all happened. It was disturbing, almost disappointing, that they hadn't lashed out in any juvenile way, spray painted the walls, taken a shit on the bed. I had been resigned to the worst. They might have even stolen, or at least smashed, the TV as a message. But it was all untouched. They only wanted me. Nice and neat.

My eyes snapped wide and I hustled down the hall and closed and locked the front door. Jesus, what if someone was watching for me? I went into the kitchen and found my pan-and-coffee-cup door chime and hung it on the knob by its shoelace, then went back to the bedroom for fresh clothes. I glanced at the clock and felt the icy fingers tracing down my spine. Twelve-fucking-thirty. I was due at work in less than two hours.

I could call in with any excuse, I knew. I could not call in and just be AWOL for all anyone would ultimately care, but…

At a quarter to two I locked the apartment behind me, checking the doorknob twice, and went down the steps into the afternoon sun. Longing to hide somewhere, to slink off and disappear, to do anything but what I was doing—stumbling down onto the walkway and making my way to my car as if I was a prison guard conducting my own self down the corridor to the gas chamber.

At five to two I parked in front of Vanguard Liquors and looked at the place with its neon OPEN sign glowing and the seedy cardboard LOTTO advertisements propped in its dust-caked windows. I wished I could reach into my chest and take hold of my heart, squeeze it hard enough to stop its wild twitching. Inside that building was the underbelly of Blackmer. Inside was my fate. I stood out of the car, imagining Sully and his friends staring at me, nudging each other and saying, "Holy shit! Sam's out of his fucking mind! He's gonna get killed!" It added a faint whiff of satisfaction to the death-march atmosphere.

I locked my car and moved. Over the blacktop, past the newspaper display rack, through the doorway. It was cool and dim inside and Sully said, "What's up, Sam," in a flat, possibly sarcastic voice. He had one friend standing across the counter from him. A Mexican gangster in a huge white T-shirt, with slicked back hair and the usual lip caterpillar.

I said, "What's up," and got an orange juice from the cooler. I deliberately said, "What's up," to the gangster and he stared a moment, then gave a single nod.

There was a used car salesman yammering from the TV in the corner. The three of us didn't say anything and

I just sipped my orange juice, again and again, a nervous tick, being careful not to slop it over my chin, hoping the two young men couldn't see how much my hand was shaking.

"Well, I'm outa here," Sully said, somehow extricating himself from everything with those words.

I kept my jacket on, although I became uncomfortably warm. Fifteen, twenty minutes passed and I stood behind the counter. Two guys came in and bought a couple of twelve packs. A guy in a suit came in and bought cigarettes. I was too distracted to bother turning off the sports program on the TV. There was something comforting about the noise and presence; about the way it had nothing to do with me, as if evidence that I wasn't Sam Schuler after all. I surveyed each customer as they approached the store, telling myself I had the advantage here—they had to enter through that thirty-inch doorway. They couldn't sneak up on me. I was positioned like the Spartans at Thermopylae. I could whip out my little revolver and start blasting away, on more or less equal terms, with whoever came at me through that door.

My cell phone began its electronic impersonation of a real phone. Ring-ring! Pause. Ring-ring! I retrieved it, saw the distantly familiar number and snapped it open. "Hello."

"Where are you, Sam?"

"Tommy!"

"Yeah, Grandpa Art just raked my ass over the coals. Thanks a lot for that, ya prick. Where you hiding out?"

"I'm at work."

"At that fucking liquor store?"

"Yeah."

"Listen." His voice sounded strange. Strained. "You're gonna get killed, Sam. I mean that literally. Some people already asked me about you. I mean some fucked up fucking people. You can't just—fuck. Lock the door and just hang out there. Lay down behind the fucking counter, why don't you. I'm coming right now."

"You're coming here?" I said, but he had hung up.

I took out my keys and moved toward the door, but Jean was there. She was a brain-damaged sixty-year-old ex-addict who came in every shift. She had bloodless, parchment skin, thinning hair with a cheap auburn dye job, and an IV bag on a roller-stand next to her. She called the IV bag and roller her "date," which I thought was funny the first dozen times she said it. She had some terminal condition and the only joy in her life was throwing away her social security money playing scratch-off lottery tickets. I think she went hungry so she could buy them. I didn't even have the chance to tell her I needed to close the store; she and her "date" had already passed the threshold and were shuffling toward the counter.

She stationed herself against the counter and began her ticket-buying spree, two, three, five at a time, selecting the different themes—Gold Rush, Luck O' The Irish, etc.—which all had the same dismal odds of paying off. Sometimes she won five bucks, sometimes two, and she always put her winnings back into more tickets. She called out the plays to me as she scratched away with her nickel—"Oh, there's two pots of gold! I just need one more!"—and I suffered this for ten minutes before I saw the car stop right in front of the door and felt my nerves melt.

I watched the stout, tough gangster—the gamecock from the other night—rise out of the passenger's side, cross the walkway and trigger the door buzzer as he stepped through the entrance. Out in the sun the driver popped up from the other side and followed. I wrapped my hand around the gun in my pocket and began to duck. Jean said, "There you go! Lookit that! Two free tickets!" and waved the thing in front of me.

Then I saw the huge, brown, rust-rotted cruise ship from 1974 heave up beside the gangsters' car and rock as the brakes were applied. It was a Plymouth or a Pontiac or something—twice the size, at least, of the Japanese vehicle. Tommy was already out and running around the hood.

"Hey!" the old woman said. "You gonna give me my tickets, honey?"

I was in a half-crouch. The gun was caught in the torn lining of the pocket of my derby. The gamecock had a gun at his side, I now saw, and he was looking at the old woman, trying to figure out if he should shoot me in front of her. Beyond him, just outside, was the skinny gangster, and my eyes traced down from his bony shoulder and I saw his gun too. His skeletal, mud-colored Indian face was taut and half-crazed with fear. The electronic beeper sounded as he finally passed into the store and in that instant the beeper sounded again and his eyes rolled up in his head and his legs turned to water. I saw Tommy lifting the length of pipe away as the skinny gangster crumpled to the floor without a sound. I jerked at the .38 now, shredding the lining of my coat, and I managed to fire it through my jacket pocket, into the shelving under the counter.

The shot seemed to shake the whole store, left the air itself quivering. "OH!" Jean said, pulling her IV bag closer to her, eyes wide and mouth sagging open.

The gamecock was now rushing at me, bug-eyed. The explosion of the gun had clearly panicked him and he whipped the big black pistol up, to just kill me, when Tommy hacked the pipe down onto the crown of his skull, causing blood to spring forth instantaneously. Tommy clubbed twice more as the man was on the way down, and I heard him muttering through clenched teeth, something about, *try to kill MY motherfucking cousin!*

I was stepping around the counter without knowing what I was doing. Jean was staring at me, still holding up her ticket that was good for two more of the same. Her mouth was an O, her eyes were huge, her face comically grotesque. At her feet now was the unconscious gangster and I watched her eyes find him.

"Come on, Sam!" Tommy barked. "Let's get the fuck out of here!" There was nothing but business in his voice. He shoved the pipe in his back pocket, bent and took Gamecock's gun, then crouched over the skinny gangster and took his gun as well, saying, "Fucking punks!"

"Oh my gaaaawd!" Jean said, but she sounded amused now.

The skinny gangster stirred and tried to sit up, and I watched in respectful awe as Tommy passed both the confiscated guns to his left hand, cocked his right fist back and neatly clipped the young man on the chin, causing him to exhale and sag flat onto the maroon mat.

"Get in your car and follow me!" he said, already beeping the door buzzer, jogging out to his car.

I hadn't even gotten the .38 out of my pocket. I looked at Jean over the two flattened gangsters and said, "Those guys were trying to kill me! I have to go!" and she astounded me by saying, "Run! Run!" and she was already dragging her IV bag toward the door after me.

I left the store open with the two gangsters in piles on the utility mats and the old lady getting herself out of there behind me. I ran straight to my car and jabbed the key into the driver's door. Tommy waited, revving his 1970s heap, shooting black smoke from under the rear bumper, staring at me and then pulling out as soon as I sat down behind my steering wheel. He chirped the tires around a row of parked cars and I cranked the ignition key and shoved the Fairlane into first and took off after him.

We had to sit at two lights and then we were hurtling

down the freeway onramp and sliding over and fitting ourselves into the fast lane traffic. I fished out my cell, found Sully's cell number after a few moments of punching buttons and darting my eyes between the gadget and the road, and punched CALL.

"Yo," Sully answered.

"Sully, man, can you go down to Vanguard and cover for me? I had to get the fuck out of there."

It was silent for a few seconds and I figured he was profoundly stoned. "Yep," he finally said. "I guess so. What happened?"

I left Tommy out of the retelling. I just told Sully two guys had come in to kill me and I had run for it. I told him that the store was just sitting there open, and if he could get down there before too much was stolen I'd owe him big. He sighed and said, "Fuck it. Sure."

I thanked him and ended the call. A few cars ahead of me, Tommy's brown Cadillac or Plymouth or whatever it was was cooking along at seventy-five, leaving a thin, black mist in its wake. I kept my eyes fastened on it and just tried to breathe.

ELEVEN

We dropped to a legal sixty-five miles per hour and
drove for about ten minutes—Tommy's brown rusty
cruise ship and my muscle car fallen from glory scudding up the highway. We hit a town called Greens Landing, a beachfront community which existed in the
netherland between quaint tourist trap and dismal slum,
featuring failing antique shops and seafood restaurants
hoping to hook tourists going between Monterey and
Del Mar.

Tommy's right turn signal began blinking through its
grime and he slowed and veered over, lifting roadside
dust, and I followed. We swung down a sidestreet with
that sunny but miserably windy and sandblasted quality
that beachtown streets sometimes have—as inviting as
the surface of Mars. Tommy swung his car hard to the

left, so the suspension rocked the frame almost to the ground, and I followed him into the back parking lot of a bar and seafood restaurant.

As he stood out of his car he dragged hard on a cigarette and then flicked it into the windswept lot. He threw his hood back, exposing his outdated blond hair and unshaven jaw and threw me a look and a "come on" jerk of the head, and passed into the back door. I recognized the place as I rose from my car. It was called The Greens Landing Jazz Club and featured smalltime local bands every weekend. I had been there once with Tommy, two years ago when I was single and on the prowl, and I remembered being badly disappointed by the prospects presented. There had been only a motley gathering of aging local types and Norse Viking bikers, shouting, playing darts and pool, dancing with their fat "old ladies" to raunchy George Thorogood covers. There was a feeling of shady deals and of the possibility of getting beat with a chain in the back lot. The bar was Tommy's second home.

The inside was dark as a moonless night, until your eyes adjusted, at which point it became only dark as a porno theater. The woman tending bar greeted Tommy like he was her brother, took his order for fish and chips and set us up with a pitcher of Busch and two glasses, which we took to a far corner booth. There was one other table occupied by a couple of workingman types, but they were all the way across the room.

"I ask her," Tommy said, throwing a look toward the

bar, "she'll commit fuckin' perjury in front of a grand fuckin' jury for me."

I raised my eyebrows, nodded.

"So we can say what we want. We got an alibi if we need it—or we got someone to say were were never here and never had this conversation."

I looked at him. His cheeks were flushed. His hands moved perpetually, fluttering through his hair, bringing his beer to his lips. His ass kept shifting as if he was sitting on broken glass. This was what happened when you banned smoking in bars. "You know," he said, "there's only one way out of this."

We looked at each other. I was blank. "What is it?" I finally said.

"You really don't know?"

"Fuck! Just help me out here, Tommy. I'm fuckin' scared."

He fired a glance toward the bar, then leaned forward. "You gotta fuckin' kill Owen Ferguson, Sam—"

"Come *on*!" I leaned back, turned my beer in my hands, took a nervous gulp, slopped some down my shirtfront.

"You fucked up, Sam. Get it through your head. Some scrap motherfucker offered me money to scare you up this morning. Fuckin' idiots. My own cousin! They told me two hundred bucks I help 'em out. Owen's put the word out, man. It's business now. Probably a thousand bucks or something, so this dude comes to me figuring I could show him where you're hiding out and he'd get to you first and clear eight hundred. Or maybe it's more, I don't know. And then you just show up for *work?*" He shook his head.

I tried not to show it but my heart had begun thundering. I wanted to pitch my head over the side of the booth and puke. This was Hollywood stuff. There was a *hit* out on me. I cleared my throat. "No shit," was all I could get out.

"No shit, Sam. So you can either run for it, or you can do something about it."

"You'll help me?" My mouth reacted almost against my will. Committing me.

Tommy scoffed and said, "What do you think I'm *doing*, asshole?" and reached over the table and shoved my shoulder almost belligerently.

"What am I supposed to do? Just go and shoot him? Go the fuck to prison?" The pitch of my voice was climbing.

"No, dumb-ass!" And then a blank and charming smile opened up on his face and he leaned back and said, "There you are!" as the barmaid set the plastic basket of fish & chips in front of us. There was a little dish of tartar sauce in the side and the grease on the breaded food shined as if it was painted on with a brush.

"What're you two so secretive about?" she said, not really caring.

"Big time deals," Tommy said. "You know me."

"Oh yeah, I'm sure," she said. She was maybe forty with whatever good looks she'd once possessed blasted off her as if by a nuclear explosion, leaving her skin dry and brown, her black hair thinned and dead. "Lemme know if you need anything else," she said, turning away.

"You know what I need!" Tommy called after her, and she laughed and actually swung her flat, fat backside as she walked back to the bar.

"Don't tell me you hit *that*," I said.

"No, Sammy, I still got pretty good vision—and sense of fuckin' smell!" he said, leaning in again. But there was no doubt in my mind he had walked away from the woman buttoning his pants at least once.

"Now listen." He was speaking around a mouthful of food, his jaws working, lips glistening. "There's no telling Grandpa Art after this one, Sam." He swallowed. "We do this shit, we get our stories straight and we never mention it again. No evidence, no nothing. We were never there." The beer in front of me had emptied somehow, leaked right through the bottom of the glass, and I filled it again from the pitcher. I was just nodding, trying to drag my consciousness to the place where it believed I could commit murder.

I was slightly drunk when my cell rang. It was Lucinda, the three-hundred-pound manager of Vanguard Liquors. She said she had called the store and discovered Sully was working instead of me and she wanted to make sure I was all right and would be able to work my next shift. Sully had told her I was sick and she asked me what was wrong. I said I had a flu bug or something; I had thrown up and my head was throbbing. She said nothing about any gangsters trying to kill me and I realized the whole episode had gone unnoted by cops or citizens, as if erased from the record of time. The gangsters must have just got up and left, wondering, literally, what had hit them. Jean, the scratcher ticket lady, might talk about it in the future, but people would probably think she had hallucinated the whole thing. As far as anyone not involved knew, I had merely gotten sick and left work early. Lucinda told me to sleep as much as I could and drink plenty of liquids and call if I wouldn't be there tomorrow. I promised I would, thanked her for understanding, and thumbed the END button.

I hung out with Tommy all day. We drank three pitchers of Busch in the Greens Landing Jazz Club but he never got drunk, and I guessed it was because he was tweaking. After a while we left to ditch my car. I followed him to a house in town and parked in the back, and then we went through a backyard like a city landfill and knocked on a door held to its frame by little more than habit. A tattered and cadaverous young man answered, shook hands with Tommy, and we hung out in his so-called home for an hour or two; he had a huge, high definition TV and we watched a show about ancient Rome on HBO while he and Tommy made a quick drug deal, then smoked crank in tin foil, then chattered at a machinegun pace and got excited whenever naked people appeared on the television screen.

As the sky beyond the smudged window turned red, Tommy said, "Hey, we gotta go. Can we leave my cousin's car in the back there?" and the cadaver said, "Sure," and continued looking at the TV, fanning the fingertips of his two hands together. It seemed Tommy might have asked if we could piss on the living room rug and the man would have said, "Sure," and continued staring at the TV and fanning his fingertips together.

In Tommy's mildew-stinking car, rolling up the street, he said, "Don't big bad Owen hang out at that bar right by your work?"

"Yeah. We gonna go *there* and get him?"

He made a ridiculous voice and said, "Now you're catchin' on, country cousin!"

"I can't walk in that fuckin' place. Neither can you. He knows you and knows we're cousins, right?"

"Calm down, Sammy. We'll go there and stake the motherfucker out. You need to watch more TV. But first we gotta get rid of this piece of shit."

So we nursed the great brown stinking cruise ship across Greens Landing and mercifully turned off the engine in front of yet another of Tommy's friends' homes.

"This is someone *you* know?" I said. This house had a fresh coat of paint on it and a landscaped little yard out front.

"She's a CPA. She helps me out."

"A certified public accountant?" I couldn't keep my voice even. "Who the fuck are you kidding—"

"She helps me with tax shit. Shut the fuck up about it, Sam."

"You haven't filed fuckin' taxes since…You've never filed fuckin' taxes in your life!"

"Hey. Sam. Fuck you."

I apologized and got out of the car with him. We went up a couple of steps to a nice Craftsman porch and knocked. The woman who answered said, "Well, hello," in a familiar way and let us into a pleasant front room with shiny hardwood floors and decent furnishings. There was a new black computer on the table in the corner with a screensaver going that was supposed to make it look like a tropical fish-tank. I was introduced and Tommy actually told her, with a straight face, that I was an amateur boxer and had just got knocked around in an exhibition bout—which I won. I just nodded and said pleased to meet you. Her name was Candy; she had iron-gray hair and mother-earth breasts. She was about fifty-five, shapely but old-looking, and I was surprised when Tommy hugged her and squeezed her ass. The whole thing began to make sense as Tommy explained to her that he hadn't been able to help missing the last meeting because his grandpa was sick. She rolled her eyes at him and he pretended not to notice. So that was it. As of Tommy's most recent parole he was forced to go to AA meetings, and there he came into contact, occasionally, with a better class of people. This woman probably never ingested any controlled substances more dangerous than half a bottle of wine at bedtime. She probably went to these meetings out of sheer loneliness—which Tommy had smelled from across the meeting hall.

Tonight he told Candy that he was fixing that brown, 1970s heap for someone, but he couldn't get parts until tomorrow so could he please borrow her car for a few hours. She immediately went for the keys, which were hanging by the door, and she chided him to not smoke in it and to bring it back before morning. Just knock and she'd get up, she said. There was no mistaking the meaning in the statement.

Tommy thanked her and I thanked her as we edged out the door, and then we were down the stairs, stepping to a perfectly clean and respectable little Ford Focus that we had no right to ride in. Tommy clicked the electronic lock as if he'd driven the car frequently and we climbed in. It smelled new and neat and Tommy said, "That's better," as we pulled away.

I began laughing in spite of myself, and Tommy said, "Not a fucking word about it, Sam. Anyway, you don't know it from how she looks in clothes, but she's got a pretty solid body."

I made chuffing noises, my hand clapped over my mouth.

"Fuck you, Sam!" Tommy said, his scowling face distorted and ugly, lit from below by the dashboard lights. "Wait and see what you're getting when you're my age."

I covered my face and said, sorry, sorry, and tried to get myself under control. Then we rolled onto Highway 1, headed north, and I felt the good humor bleed from me. My insides stretched to spring-loaded tension and I blinked out at the headlights washing over the asphalt in front of us. It was Saturday night and we were going to Rancho Bonita, where, if this was like most nights, Owen Ferguson would be holding court in the barroom.

TWELVE

Fifteen minutes later we were parked in the Baron Square Shopping Center and it was enjoying an evening rush. The drug store and the grocery store were still open and people bustled to and from cars, pushing carts, trailing children. The liquor store was lit up and I could see Sully through the glass, in the lighted interior, as clear and obvious as a performer in a spotlight at the front of a blackened theater. I thought of how that could have been me in there tonight, and how anyone could have sat outside, taken aim, and just shot me in the head as I lingered over the cash register. It made me a little sick.

We parked in a span of empty spaces, removed from other cars and foot traffic. I could look in at Vanguard Liquors to my right, and see the bar entrance of Rancho Bonita to my left. "What now?" I said.

"What now?" Tommy echoed. "We need to find out if your fuckin' boyfriend is in there."

"I doubt he is," I said, thinking about it. "He and his friends probably won't come here until ten or so." The dash clock said 8:32.

"Well, fuck," Tommy said, lighting a cigarette and hitting the button so a little motor hummed and the door sucked down the glass of the window. "We just gotta sit here and wait."

And we did. I tried to engage Tommy in conversation and discovered he wouldn't say two words about anything that might in some way qualify him as a human being. I wanted to get a feel for what was happening here tonight. How people did these lunatic things and what it would mean in my life from this day forward. But Tommy just wanted to chain smoke and make jokes, which got old pretty fast and led to long silences when I didn't laugh. His favorite subject, I found, was himself twenty years before when he had, by his account, fucked every girl in this county, and most of the eligible girls in California. I tried to steer us to something more meaningful, asking him about Grandpa Art, who was the closest thing to a father either of us had, and he said "Yep," and nothing more. I asked him if Grandpa Art was actually tough back in the day and Tommy perked up and spoke with respect, saying, "He was one of those guys. He didn't say much, but you didn't want to rile that motherfucker. He'd smack the fuck out of you." He followed with a story I found deeply fascinating, about

Grandpa Art as a much younger man and Tommy as a ten-year-old. The two of them were waiting in line to ride the roller coaster at the Boardwalk and as they stood there a girl had sprinted up, glancing behind her, and ruptured the line and burst through. A second later a massive young man came in pursuit of her, and Grandpa Art—who was then about forty—had kicked the angry boyfriend's foot so it hooked behind his other ankle and he sprawled on the pavement. My granddad had then circled and dodged with the outraged youth and landed a punch that sat the boy down on his ass. The show had continued until the police arrived a minute later and arrested the boyfriend.

I can't say why this meant anything to me, but it did. It was a window into these two people's pasts—Tommy as a kid, Grandpa Art as a man at the height of his powers. I was struck by the strange pathos of it. The sharp kid Tommy once was, the potential to be anything, reduced to this lying, scheming shipwreck of a human being beside me. The casually capable man Grandpa Art had been, now forced to tiptoe along the edge of the high cliffs where one day, inevitably, he'd lose footing, his heart would freeze and he'd just tumble off into nothing. Christ, why bother with anything? I was on that same conveyer belt of time and shitty luck, no better than Tommy or Grandpa Art, being delivered to oblivion sooner or later—

"What's he drive?"

"What?"

"Your fuckin' boyfriend."

"Oh...Shit...It's a...uh...Celica! A Toyota. It's white. Lowered."

"Idn't that him?" Tommy gestured toward the liquor store with his cigarette and I snapped my head to my right. The shape, the *personality* of that little white Celica was tattooed on my brain. It spelled menace for me because with it, of course, was Owen. I felt the pressure in my chest. He had pulled up to the curb and parked right in front of the door of Vanguard. He was out of his car and just passing inside. I imagined the door buzzer going off as I watched him stroll up to Sully in the brightness, lean across the counter and perform the postmodern handshake—hand clasp, palm slap, knuckle bump—and then place both hands on the countertop and begin talking. I looked at his hard narrow back and wondered, just wondered, if he was asking Sully where I might be tonight. I saw Sully shake his head as he spoke.

"He's looking for me," I said.

"Probably." Tommy leaned forward, lifting his hand to the keys that dangled in the ignition.

"What're you doing?"

He dragged on his cigarette so the cherry lit up. He exhaled and squinted through the smoke. "To tell you the truth, Sammy, I don't fuckin' know. Just sit tight and let's see what happens."

Tommy started the car as Owen turned and walked out of Vanguard. It felt like too much was happening too fast. I was short of breath. We backed out, then dropped into drive and crawled across the parking lot, our eyes fastened on the taillights of the little Celica.

"Maybe we'll find out where the fucker lives," Tommy said.

We wove through the nighttime city behind him, as if there was an invisible tow rope connecting his back bumper to our front. Streetlights slid up and passed. Headlights floated toward us and vanished. When the latter shone through the glass of Owen's car, we saw that there was someone in the passenger seat. I didn't really know what Owen Ferguson did on a Saturday night, but I imagined he was furious about what had happened this afternoon so he had paired himself with some incredible badass who was graffitied from head to toe in prison tattoos and the two of them were bent on finding and killing me before morning. Then I imagined that I was a fool, exaggerating my importance in the scheme of Owen's life—he couldn't care less about me and he and this passenger were just doing whatever they did, picking up and delivering drugs, I guessed.

Headlights came through his glass again and I noted the shape of their heads, Owen's tall and narrow, his passenger's round and squat as a jack-o'-lantern.

"No way," I said, feeling sick as we turned onto Tuttle Avenue.

We slowed to a crawl, and I watched Owen's car swing into the parking lot without signaling.

"Isn't this—" Tommy said, and I said, "Yeah. This is my fucking apartments."

"Get out your gun," Tommy said, and he was reaching inside his sweatshirt.

"What? No. Fuck."

He jammed the Ford into a parking space at the curb and killed the engine. Some residual, bluish light played on his face, shined on his eyeballs as he turned to me. "Sam, you little fuck. This is your fucking chance, you prick. We catch 'em in your place, it's a home fuckin' invasion and we kill the motherfuckers. Bam! Bam!" He was wild-eyed now, psyching himself up for this. I saw the big gun in his hand.

"Where'd that come from?" I said.

"Where do you think? Those punks at the store, dipshit. This's a Glock, like cops use. My fuckin' favorite. Now come on."

Tommy elbowed the door open and got out of the car. "Hurry up!" he said and I sucked a breath and got out myself. We pushed the doors shut just hard enough to latch them and kill the interior lights.

The parking lot of the apartment complex was small, and many tenants parked on the street. Depending on who was at work when, you could find and use empty spaces, but it was understood that you were in someone else's slot and they'd be upset if they came off a long shift and found your car there. They might key your doors, and they'd be in keeping with the unwritten rules. Tommy and I moved under a covered area, between front bumpers, both of us with guns in our hands. I felt like a Boy Scout tracking game with Davey Crockett.

The Celica was plain as day, parked beside the furthest apartment building next to the NO PARKING sign. Both its doors stood open and rap music bumped from the door speakers. Tommy came close to me and breathed sweet liquor breath across the side of my face as he whispered: "Let's see what they do. They ain't staying here long. Maybe they're dropping off some shit, or making a pickup."

Shit, I knew, meant drugs of one kind or another.

"Wait a minute!" Tommy's face was intense with inspiration. He jerked his hand out of his sweatshirt pocket, took the wrist of my left hand, and slapped the car keys into it. He then whapped me on the shoulder hard enough so I stumbled a step forward. "You follow us!"

"Follow who?" But he was running across the murky blacktop toward the Celica, a large, bulky silhouette barreling ahead in a crouch, moving with surprising speed. I saw his big white paw crawling madly, groping at the side of the front seat until he found the lever and the seat folded forward, and then he pitched himself into the back. I saw the disembodied hand come forward again, find the same lever and return the driver's seat to its upright position. I breathed, "Holy fuck!" out loud. The man was insane. I knew now what was happening. They would climb back into their car and he would make some glib comment like, "Evening, gentlemen," or maybe just, "Drive where I tell you, motherfucker, or you're dead," and he'd have that gun cocked at the backs of their heads.

I ran. Slipping between car fronts, then out to the street and back to the Ford Focus. I had the sensation of being jerked out of the moment, looking down at myself, astounded at what I was doing. I had to force myself to keep moving, to act, to just do this and not stop to think. I pushed the key into the ignition and started the car, noticing how quiet the motor was compared to the sick rumble of my Fairlane. Ford had made a little progress, at least, in forty-five years.

I didn't twist the lights on. I started to drop it into drive, but didn't do that either because then I would have to put a foot on the brakes and ignite the brake lights. But then, Owen and this other gangster would have Tommy, a huge, drunk, tweaking maniac pointing a gun at their heads. What did they care if some asshole they drove by had his fucking foot on the brake? I dropped it into drive and did a three point turn so I was ready to follow. Maybe a minute passed, then I saw backup lights coming toward me out of the parking lot. It was the Celica. This was happening.

The car reversed soberly, hooking out of the lot and onto the street, then the backup lights went dark and it started moving. I fell in behind it, my chin thrust over the steering wheel, trying but failing to envision what might be playing out with three violent men penned inside that little metal capsule. But the streetlights bounced back at me off the window glass and I could see nothing. This part of town was too bright for making out black shapes in the glare of oncoming headlights.

I had to sleeve the sweat off my forehead and I muttered a long unbroken monologue about how fucked I was and how insane this was, but my gaze was fastened to the Celica's taillights and I matched its speed and trailed along right behind it. We went to the edge of town, broke out of the last lighted intersection and sped up to cruising speed on the 129—which is a dark state highway that draws a long, arcing line between highway 1 and highway 101. They did the speed limit and I followed, still cursing. About two miles out I gasped as the Celica veered into the middle of the road, then the brake lights flared up and it eased right and came to a stop at the shoulder. I applied my foot to the Ford's brake pedal and stopped behind it.

I spoke aloud, saying, *"What the fuck what the fuck what the fuck!"* The Celica didn't move. Just sat idling on the shoulder. Then the brake lights went dark and it eased forward again and I pushed the gas and continued to follow.

Another mile and we turned right onto a road called Murphy's Crossing, which was another shortcut, this time between the 129 and San Gabriel Road. I had a premonition then, knowing this pass led only to a small community and dozens of agricultural tracts, and was used very little after dark. The stretch crossed the Conejo River, and in its middle was a cement bridge that carried cars over the secretive jungle foliage of the river's bank.

As I knew we would, we slowed and stopped before we reached the bridge. The Celica turned right without signaling, nosing up onto a farm road, folding tall grass under its lowered undercarriage. I nosed up behind it, the car looking somehow ominous, somehow obscene, removed from the pavement, washed by my white headlights. I watched as Owen opened the driver's door and stood out of his car. He squinted back at me for a moment. He was keeping his hands in the open. And then I watched the gun emerge after him, followed by Tommy's arm, and then Tommy himself unfolded, the same height as Owen but twice the gangster's width. Where was the other gangster? I didn't have time to contemplate the question because Tommy was glaring at me, jerking his arm toward himself, waving me over. I pushed the gear lever into park, killed the engine and got out, but Tommy was shaking his head. "Lights! Turn 'em off!"

I turned off the lights and moved toward them. As soon as I was near, Owen said, "Schuler! You're fucking up, Homes!" his voice somewhere between threatening and begging.

I didn't answer. Tommy had turned out the Celica's headlights and closed the door so its interior lights were dark. The three of us stood under the moonlight like nocturnal animals.

"I didn't go anywhere near your chick, man. You're fucking up!" Owen said, his voice getting slightly shrill.

I looked at Tommy and said, "What if he didn't?"

Owen's eyes locked with mine and he looked like just a kid—blinking, swallowing, trying to appeal to me without words.

But Tommy was shaking his head again. He said, "Look inside the car, Sam," in a flat voice. "Hey!" he added. "Put your sleeve over your fingers. No fingerprints."

I did as he said, opening the driver's door of the Celica with my jacket sleeve hooked over my fingers. The dome light shined on the other gangster. It was the gamecock. His cap was pushed up, so it was on top of his head but he wasn't wearing it. He was twisted and bent forward, his temple against the dash. His eyes were blank and the brain and blood and bone that the bullet had accumulated as it tore through his head was spattered on the interior of the window glass around him.

I inhaled and now caught the faint butcher shop smell and stood straight. I closed the door with my knee. I looked at Tommy and said, "Fuck!" in a weak voice.

"You don't want to finish this?" Tommy said. "After all this you don't want to take out the motherfucker that raped your girlfriend?"

"Fuck, Tommy!" My heart seemed to shake my whole body. "Just hang on! Really, what if I fucked up?"

"Listen, Sam!" Owen's Mexican accent was thicker than ever, his jaw seemed to jut out to a painful level, as if he spent all his life trying to keep his underbite under control and now, panicked, he couldn't stop it from thrusting out an inch more than usual. His eyebrows were knit hard and his nostrils flaring. His eyes were wet, but I didn't believe they were actually tearing up. "Schuler!" he said. It came out as if he was ordering me.

"I wouldn't rape your chick, Homes! Think about it. That ain't my style and you know it! I never heard about any of this shit until your cousin—"

You never realize how loud a gunshot is from watching movies. In the nanosecond during the explosion all other sound in the universe is drowned out and every cell in your body convulses, shudders, shrinks back.

The bullet passed through the side of Owen's head and flesh and bone sprayed out the other side before the head could even lean in the direction of the shot. Owen's body went down to the knees, then flopped into the tall grass almost slowly, almost easily, like a kid pretending to die in a game of cops and robbers.

Tommy stood stock still for a long moment, gun still extended.

Then he snapped out of it. He stepped backward, turned and jabbed the gun into the back pocket of his jeans. He pulled his sweatshirt over his head so his T-shirt slid up and his thick pale torso shone in the moonlight. He used the sweatshirt as a rag and wiped where he had touched the side of the seat and the adjustment lever, then climbed in back like an animal squeezing into its burrow. I could hear him huff air onto surfaces, fogging them like a person does glass, and then wiping them down. He emerged again from the driver's side, using his forearms for support, careful not to put his hands on anything. He stepped over to me and said, "Gimme the keys. Let's go."

His face was shiny. His body odor powerful now. I

found the keys in my pocket and laid them in Tommy's palm.

"We're not gonna do anything else? Hide them?" I said as he walked past me.

"Nope. Get in. Hurry up," he said, sitting in the driver's side of the Ford Focus.

There had been no traffic on the road. I thought of all the detective stories I had read, about the cops finding tire tracks, but we had driven on either tall grass or dry hard dirt.

"Cops couldn't ever dream who iced those fuckin' idiots," Tommy said as if he was reading my mind. "There's no pattern, no nothing. Don't think about all that Detective Columbo bullshit, Sam. It's over. They're gonna look at this shit and shrug. Figure some drug deal gone fucked up. And I used one of their guns, too. There's nothing. Listen. Just never think about this shit again. Never talk about it to anyone, you hear me?"

"I hear you." I was wondering if Tommy had done this sort of thing frequently in the past, but not really wanting to know.

As we drove back to Greens Landing Tommy said, "I need a shower." And I grunted and said, "I'd say so." The events beside the river were broken off clean by Tommy's willing it to be so. He had advised me to forget it, and now was leading the way.

"See that?" he said. "And I got a shower waiting. You make fun of Candy, but look, we got this car to use, I can use her shower…"

"Her body," I offered.

"Even that, asshole. I ain't too good to take one for the team. What—do you think that's all I get?"

"Naw," I said, "There's that supermodel at the bar today."

"Fuck you, Sam. I never hit that. Shit, I fuck girls that you'd wet your fuckin' pants if they said hello to you."

I couldn't help but scoff and I said, "Yep, that's exactly my point."

He was quiet for a moment, then muttered, "See what kind of pussy you're getting when you get my age, you fuckin' punk."

There was menace in his voice, and I thought of him killing people and said, "I'm just kidding, Tommy. Jesus, I thought you could take a joke."

He said nothing and I continued:

"Hey, I want to say thanks for helping me out. Seriously." I cleared my throat and looked at his face, glowing from the miniature footlights on the dashboard. "You saved my life."

And he sighed, one of his rare human moments, and said, "Yeah," in a defeated way.

THIRTEEN

An hour later, back in my car, I could only think of Jill. My longing for her, for the life and the new family she represented, was suddenly overpowering. I tried to delve down to the source of the impulse and could only equate it with the men coming back from war, returned from seasons of cold and slaughter and the abiding threat of death and now able to truly appreciate the comforts of hearth and home and the creation and nurturing of life. How lucky I am, how unbelievably fucking lucky, I thought at long last, that this baby was coming and that I had a girl like Jill for my own.

I glanced at my cell and it wasn't even midnight yet. I punched in the number of Jill's mother's house. It rang and rang and the muscles of my neck and shoulders hardened. Oh Jesus. I had set the whole of gangland on edge, I had gotten them angry enough to take steps to kill me…would they go after Jill? Couldn't they research, ask around, find out where her mother lives and go wait for her, drag her into a car or something? "Please, God," I said aloud. "Let her be fine."

"Sam?" Jill said, sounding sleepy.

"How'd you know?" I said.

"Caller ID. We gotta get it when…whenever we move to a new place. It's great." She paused, then said, "Sam? I've been having nightmares about you getting killed or something. I don't know why."

A shiver went up my spine. "No such luck," I said. "I'm coming over, all right?"

She waited a moment. "Yes. Hurry up."

We ended the call and I set the cell on the seat beside me. I wanted to tell Jill the whole story but I shook my head. Never. What if she could never see me the same? Wanted nothing to do with me? And that was nothing. What if she repeated the story in confidence, to a girl-friend, who then repeated it to someone else and so on until the cops came knocking? No, I would have to lock it up inside me and carry it with me for the rest of my life.

It couldn't be difficult, I thought. Men went off to war for years, did and saw things that should not enter the life and mind of any civilized person. This was nothing. A few days of my life—I realized that since the time Rich had crawled in my car and I had smelled the pot it had been exactly a week. Seven days. A brief disruption of the natural order, an infection flaring up, burning, raging, and then dying with those two brutal gunshots. Now the wounds would scab over, the scar tissue would form and life would continue.

And I finally let Owen Ferguson step to center stage in my mind. I replayed his last moments, then rewound and replayed them again. He was nearly begging. Well, how would he act, anyway? Of course he would say he didn't do it, but…My stomach sucked up under my ribs and I could have vomited. My palms were sweaty, slippery on the steering wheel. I thought of Owen looking like the kid he had never been. Confused. Genuinely terrified. I thought of his tone and I just couldn't believe he had raped anyone no matter how hard I argued the case to myself. I had known it there, beside the river, but it was no use with Tommy already having shot the other guy. And Tommy was right, after all. We weren't doing this anymore because of any rape. We were doing it because Owen was going to have me killed, or was going to kill me himself. It hadn't been revenge, it had been survival.

Sunday passed in tranquility. Jill and I took in a matinee and looked at a couple of apartments for rent in Del Mar, where the square footage was a third less and the monthly rent a third more. I slept at Jill's mother's, on a futon with Jill, in the room she had used for two or three of her teenage years.

Monday morning I went back to our apartment to shower and change clothes. I didn't bother with the door chimes, although I kept the .38 on the bathroom counter while I showered. For the first time, entranced by rain sound and the warm water massaging the back of my neck, I felt the weight and significance of what I—well, what Tommy—had done. I felt the void left by Owen Ferguson's death. The screaming silence. The engine of retribution, I realized, had been stilled. I thought of Owen's mother and little sister, and of Ramón, and wondered if they were thinking of me.

At two I stepped into Vanguard again. Another kid who worked there, Keith, said hello to me, grabbed his jacket and a pack of smokes from the rack, and left.

The entire shift ticked by, second by second, without incident. The door buzzer sounded regularly and regular customers made their regular purchases, faces I didn't know hovered before me as I rang them up, then drifted out, but nothing out of the ordinary took place. I had forgotten my book so, during the long, tedious stretch between about eight-thirty and closing I dragged the utility mats outside and beat them against a support post and piled them next to the door. I found the old broom in the back and swept the dust bunnies and heaps of dirt from all the corners of the store and transferred it to the garbage can by the door. On a high shelf in the back room I found new mop heads in plastic bags and I replaced the ancient, moldy gray head that had been on the mop since I started working here. I fixed up hot mop water, with plenty of Simple Green and a dash of bleach, and went to work. Halfway through the job the water was so filthy that I dumped it and started over. At the end I stood and surveyed my work, breathing the bleach, trying to appreciate the darkened floor mats, and sheen on the speckled tiles. It still looked like shit and I laughed to my-self, knowing that nobody who worked here would no-tice, and it would be a year before anyone thought to mop the floor again. But, what the hell, I had killed an hour.

I went through the closing ritual, darkened and locked the store, went to my car, sat while it warmed up and then drove to Del Mar to spend the night with Jill.

It wasn't until the following night that it happened.

I was beginning to feel rather confident and relaxed by seven-thirty on Tuesday, and that was when I looked up to the sound of the door buzzer and figured I was go-ing to die. The gangster was staring at me as he cruised in, his face smug. He was short, maybe forty, wearing the crisp white T-shirt and black, new workpants. He was a *veterano*, a creature of the prison systems. He had his hair slicked straight back, the teardrop tattooed next to his eye, the cursive on his neck, the murky prison ink like elaborate bruising, giving a green tincture to his brown arms. He stared at me openly as he walked in and said, "What's up, Sam Schuler?" as he passed. My heart was jumping. I turned my head and watched him strut to the beer cooler. He came back with a twelve pack of Corona in bottles, hoisted it and clinked it on the counter be-tween us. He kept staring at me as I rang the beer in and recited the price. He slid a twenty over the counter with tattooed fingers and said, "Relax, bro."

"Do I know you?"

He leaned in. "I know *you*, Homes." His skin was gray-ish-brown, his face had an oriental cast. He was smirking. "You're a badass. You're like that dude in *Death Wish*, ain't you?"

We stared at each other.

"Breathe, man," he said. "I ain't gonna do nothing to you. Word to the wise, though." His voice dropped and he leaned a little closer. "I'm the shot-caller and I already said to drop it. Someone fucked with my chick? I'd bury 'em, too, *ese*. I'll tell you the truth, I respect that. You got heart. And between you and me? A lot of people didn't like Owen and his crew. Lotta people thought they were punks, aye. So, 'officially'"—he actually made little quote marks with the fingers of his left hand—"there's no beef no more. But them two guys had some friends, and I can't guarantee you nothing. All I'm saying is, you made your point, now you want to be watching your fuckin' back."

I nodded and said, "Okay," trying to be the character he had superimposed on me—trying to be as stony-faced as Charles Bronson. I slowly unwrapped my fingers from the .38 and removed my hand from my pocket. I hit the CASH button and made his change and asked him if he needed a bag and he said nope and grabbed the twelve pack. "Take it easy, Sam," he said on his way out.

"You too," I said.

I tried to let the tension drain away. I could feel the sweat in my armpits. I wondered what had been said. I wondered if they had any idea that it had been Tommy and not me—that I wasn't anything even approaching a badass. But I couldn't guess how my reprieve had come about, what conversations had taken place in little houses and apartments in the seedy parts of town. The nerve centers of the monster, the machinations that determined its actions and decisions were unknowable to me. The monster was rabid, untamable, half insane, and it had simply turned on me one day. I had fought it, clinched with it, felt its muscles rolling and flexing beneath its dry, hot, mangy hide even as its teeth had sunk into my neck. I might have succumbed, but the secret is that the monster is not merely ferocious, it's starving and frightened and it bares its teeth and lashes out because it hopes to scare you off without a fight. I had been equally frightened, and in my desperation I had bit back. I had made it bleed and yelp, made it feel respect, at least for a moment. So now it was slinking off again, into the piss-stinking alleyways and sidestreets, in search of easier prey. It was done. It was over.

But it wasn't.

As I was stocking the beer cooler, during the last hour, I heard the door buzzer and went out behind the counter and was confronted by the sight of Rich. His face had calmed from his beating, although it was far from normal. I thought of Owen, of his near-begging, and I stared at Rich Channing.

"What's up, Sam?" he said, tilting his head, looking at my face. "So they got you too, huh? Shit, that's nothing.

You didn't even get no stitches, did you? Compared to me you look like you been in a fuckin' pillow fight…Hey, you hear about Owen Ferguson, dude?"

"Yeah, I heard."

"Is that fucked up or what? Lucky for us, though."

"Yeah," I said. The bruises on his face were a washed-out yellow. His black-stitched lip had returned to almost normal size. Except for a few scars and a little dental work he'd be himself again in another week or two and wouldn't give this incident so much as a backward glance. He looked at me looking at him and said, "What, dude?"

"Nothing," I said. I looked past him, out the door, and saw the car. The little red Japanese go-cart with the gray-primered fender. "Who's driving you around, Rich?"

"My friend. Some dude you don't know."

"What's his name?"

"Johnny."

"Yeah, I know him," I said. "Mexican dude, right? Dark skinned guy?"

His eyes went hard and he said, "Yeah, he's pretty dark, I guess." Then he recovered and said, "Hey, can I get a pack of smokes, dude? I'll pay—"

"Nope."

"What?"

"You got no money, Rich, then get the fuck out of here."

"What, dude?"

"Get the fuck out of here, Rich. Or I'm gonna come

around this fucking counter and put your face through the fucking window glass."

The fear flickered in his eyes, then dimmed. He was walking backward, and he said, "All right, dude. All right. Whatever," and he spun and almost walked into the doorjamb, grabbed onto it and steered himself out the door, making the buzzer sound again.

I walked around the counter and stepped to the doorway, staring as they drove away. My vision strained at the license plate of the little go-cart and I said the numbers and letters to myself and went inside, grabbed a pen, ripped off a piece of paper bag and wrote them down. I put the piece of paper in my wallet.

I went through my closing ritual and sat in my car as it warmed up. I looked at the dark store and it came to me, all at once, that I wasn't going to work there anymore. I would call Lucinda tomorrow and tell her-…something. It would come to me. The gangster had given me a friendly warning and this time I would listen. I had pushed the thing as far as I could, I had walked into enemy fire and found myself still alive, completely intact, marveling at my ridiculous luck. Now, if I had an ounce of brains I would retreat. I wasn't going to stand under those lights another night, waiting to see if I would draw more fire. I was going to leave town after all. But first…

FOURTEEN

Three months flew away in a moment. They were happy times for the most part. Jill and I found a one room apartment in Del Mar and I walked onto a construction site back in Blackmer, where a new movie theater was going up, and got a job cleaning up lumber scraps for ten bucks an hour. Then the foreman called me over and said to show him how I used a skillsaw, so I did, and he had me cut fifty studs down to ninety inches. Then he gave me an old tool belt and lent me a hammer and had me nail metal straps for a day, so the building wouldn't fall over in an earthquake. Then he had me frame in a small closet in the theater's office, inspected my work, and bumped my pay to fourteen dollars an hour and found another grunt to keep the jobsite clean.

By then Jill had begun showing, of course, and I had

begun worrying her. On certain nights I didn't come home after work. Grandpa Art was quite sick by then, and I would stop in once or twice a week and have dinner with him and my Grandmother since I was in town. I stayed at their house late, usually, talking about nothing and everything with my grandfather, hoping to give him the impression, by my presence, that his life had meant something. For his part he said frequently that he would remain alive at least until my child was born, but I had trouble entirely believing it.

I left after eleven usually, but on these nights I never went directly home. I took to parking my car on Valencia Street, pulling a knit cap down to my eyebrows and making excursions into the part of Conejo that lies just across the bridge, just a short walk from the burgeoning homeless encampment. In the thick of night these bars and alleys are something lower than an underbelly of this town; they are the underbelly's lower regions, its unwashed, vermin-ridden groin. This is where the smokers of chiva—black tar Mexican heroin—live out the high points of their days. If you have the nerve to push open the door and order a beer in the decayed barrooms—as I once did—you can spot them pretending happiness like ghosts reliving lost moments of pleasure, their waxy gray faces shimmering with the sick neon light. This is where inhuman appetites are gorged, where the ten dollar whores turn ten tricks a night, not even bothering to cover their scab-riddled arms. It's a never-cleaned filter, accumulating the lost souls from Mexico, the people who came to work the fields and fell to depression and disgrace, their bodies rancid, their faces horrid, puffy and purple with alcohol, their brains eaten to pieces by hard cheap drugs.

I had heard that Rich was a full-fledged addict now. He had fallen, fallen, fallen and finally struck rock bottom here, wallowing in the filth of it for endless, sleepless nights and crawling out again in daylight, materializing half sober in bars in more reputable parts of town or finding his way back to his father's, where he'd beg or steal money and catch a shower every week or two. The degeneration had been rapid, and I liked to think that his beating from Owen and my turning on him had somehow nudged him over the edge, into that final freefall, but that wasn't the case. His descent, I knew, had begun at some point when his personality was being formed; his trajectory was set back in childhood with loneliness, neglect and corruption, and his course wasn't going to be altered by any chance encounter this late in the game.

But his course could be ended.

I was not surprised when I saw him—and then I was. He was slinking out of a tiny, windowless place with a tattered green awning and a handmade sign next to the door that read El Gato Feliz—The Happy Cat. He had his arm slung over the shoulders of a creature that was supposed to be a woman but wasn't. It was a special animal that flourished in these blocks, the low-budget she-male with a purple dress from the discount store that only accentuated its bulky shoulders, and a ratty, frazzled bleach-blonde hairdo that was appalling as it framed that dark, Neanderthal face with its large shaded jaw.

I turned away as they crossed the street, and listened to them communicate across the language barrier, Rich using his few dozen words of Spanish, the shemale nodding and answering with a grotesque, girlishly-inflected broken English. "Yes, *mijo*, I *have!* I *have!*" it said and Rich said, "Okay, okay. Just making sure, *bonita*. I need it. *Yo necisito mucho!*"—I need it very much.

I swung along after them, hands in pockets, feet kicking out like any guy on an evening stroll. But my eyes were attached to, crawling all over, the backs of their heads. They crossed the street, walked over the bridge and then cut right, down off the sidewalk and onto a dirt trail that snaked toward the levee. It was a chilly night with a dome of thick, dark clouds over the city, and the shemale tried to snug itself up against Rich and he actually squeezed it against him like he was fond of it. Contrasted with the short, stout frame, Rich's long legs and good proportions were evident. It was an old, old story, I realized. He was prostituting himself for a fix. They were walking faster and faster and I knew their business was to hunker down in some secluded place and break out a hypodermic needle. Get Rich into his heroin euphoria while the shemale did God-knew-what to him.

I looked behind me, I was thirty or forty yards from the sidewalk now and I broke into a run. My fist was wrapped around the brass knuckles and my vision jolted up and down with each loping step. The dark shapes drew up, flew at me. I felt myself enter their world, saw them become aware of my presence, stop and turn, but I had already cocked my arm back and was yelling, "Police! *La policia!*"

Rich went down from the blow, crumpling onto his face in the tall grass, and the shemale turned to me, still doing its impression of a woman, eyes wide, voice simpering. *"Vete!"* I said. *"Vete de aqui, maricon! Yo soy policia!"* and it nodded, turned around, and moved down the trail in an open, manly sprint.

I stood over Rich. Waiting. My chest rose and fell. Cars whooshed over the bridge behind me but I knew nobody could see us. There was nobody else in the world. I kicked his leg. He stirred and rolled over, his hand clutching the back of his head.

"It's me Sam, Rich. Sam Schuler."

"Sam," he said. "What the fuck. Did you—?" He had sat up now. He was still holding the back of his head, giving a little shudder from time to time as if trying to shake off cobwebs. His face, as much as I could make it out, looked the same. I could see it was clean shaven by the highlight on his jaw. His black hair was parted and shiny. It occurred to me that he had prettied himself up to trade his body for a fix.

"Jill," I said.

"What?" Now he looked up, blinking with all the muscles of his face.

"My girlfriend, Jill. You went to my apartment, you and your friend. Don't even fuckin' try to tell me you didn't."

"Fuck," he said. "Dude, you're living in the past—"

I hadn't known I was going to kick him until the toe of my tennis shoe dug into his eyebrow ridge. The anger was a hot orange thing that filled me up in a heartbeat. He toppled over backward and held his face, then rolled and finally pushed himself up on his hands and knees, positioned like he was going to get up and run down the trail.

"How's *that?*" I said like an idiot. "Is *that* living in the past?"

He stayed down there before me. His breathing was loud. He didn't move. He said, "Sam, that shit, you know, it wasn't my idea. My friend, Johnny, he was all about it so I went along with it, you know what I mean?"

"You knew where I lived. He didn't. So *you* went along with taking some piece of shit to my place, and you—*you* went along with raping my fucking girlfriend?" The rage was flaring up again, I was almost choking on it.

Rich was sitting on his legs now, he had turned and was looking up at me, still rubbing his eye. He said, "Listen, dude. I know how you feel—" and I almost laughed and it dawned on me that there wasn't quite a real person inhabiting his body anymore. The drugs had left him detached from the rest of humanity, semi-retarded even. He didn't know when he was or wasn't making sense.

"—I mean," he said, "I fuckin' *liked* Jill, you know? And when that happened…Oh, no, you're not doing *that.*"

There wasn't going to be any remorse from Rich. He

wasn't going to feel the jagged, tearing teeth of Jill's tragedy and horror, or mine. Just the tragedy and horror of his own death. I had the .38 pointed at his forehead.

"Sam!" he said. "This is me here—Rich Channing, dude! Junior high, man. Fucking second period break, remember? You always bought me shit, remember? Remember snagging all that shit from the Vietnamese store?"

I centered the barrel and he didn't flinch.

He said, "I'm your *friend*, Sam!" and I shot him through the bridge of his nose and watched him go over. Then, as I'd read in some crime book, I cocked the gun again, went to one knee and placed it over his heart and fired again. The shots were everything and then they were gone and my ears were ringing. I looked up the trail to the bridge and saw nobody. The trail down to the levee was empty as well. I stood up and started walking, throwing one last glance. Rich was like part of the earth, like clothing stuffed with rags flung out onto the damp ground. I began running through the grass. following the river to where I could connect with the next street, where I would walk, slowly, easily, back to my car and drive home.

FIFTEEN

This is how the whole thing ended:

Rich had an accomplice and I had the guy's license plate number and first name—Johnny—but I didn't have the heart to seek him out. If I had known more, if I could think of some direct, logical course of action, I might have been more inclined to pursue it. But Johnny the rapist was just a few odd scraps of information, another faceless subhuman predator in a jungle full of them. Day by day the impulse toward blood-letting waned, and only occasionally did I lie awake, conscious of Jill's mountainous belly beside me, and curse myself for not hunting the motherfucker down.

The truth is, I almost let it go. I almost let him get away with it. I might have never gone back to Blackmer again if it wasn't for Grandpa Art.

And the little people.

Grandma Anne called me one Sunday, said I should come over soon, but wouldn't say why. The construction job had ended and it had been, I realized—wincing with guilt—nearly two months. I had developed a mild terror of the visits. Living and working—now at the Chevron on 33rd Avenue—in a different town, with Jill's pregnancy marching toward completion, I had walled myself off from the reality of my grandfather's decline. If you've been forced into the company of the very old, with their failing bodies and minds, you may know what a dreaded prospect it can become. You may understand how an afternoon visit can feel like three or four hours of your life being amputated in slow motion, with a dull saw.

But really, when you're all these people have, there's no excuse.

I got there in the late afternoon. It was fall now and the heater was cranked so the house's interior was at oven temperatures. I was yanking my coat off, half panicked by the sudden tropical climate as soon as the door closed behind me. I hung the coat up, cursing, and then I saw him hunched in his armchair under the front window and I felt those uncontrollable chills you get sometimes when listening to ghost stories.

He looked like the near-corpse that special effects artist concoct for certain movie scenes—scenes where the aging process is accelerated to a year a second until the figure begins decomposing before your eyes, crumbling to dust and finally blowing away.

He wasn't moving. I stepped closer, wondering if he could be dead already. He wore one of his signature T-shirts. A sun-bleached pale green thing I knew well, with peeling letters spelling out, "I'm not arrogant, I'm just better than you." His body was hardly more than a skeleton underneath it. The chalky flesh of his arms sagged like popped balloons and his face was a caricature of an old, old man, thrust forward, mute, the wrinkles gathered on top of each other and deeper than ever before.

It was a slow panic I felt. My eyes stinging, my throat constricting, my heart shocked. I dropped to one knee, placed a hand on his white-fuzzed wrist.

The ragged eyebrows shifted upward, the rinsed-out eyes found me.

"Hello, Sam."

Christ, it was so much like a corpse speaking that I almost drew my hand away. But I cleared my throat and met his gaze.

"Hey, Grandpa Art. How have you been?"

He grunted. "Just great. Just great." He had a heart-breaking slur, and I swallowed at a growing lump. " 'Cept your grandmother thinks I'm going crazy. She doesn't hear them. She doesn't see them." He made a dismissive gesture.

"Doesn't see who?"

His eyes sharpened and he studied me. He said, "Now you're not gonna turn on me too, are you? Not you, Sam! They're right there! You see that?" He pointed to the entryway of the hall. "The son of a bitches just went into my goddamned office. That's what they do when you come around, or when your grandmother comes around. They go inside the goddamned computer. Or, you may not believe it, but they dive right down the heating vents."

"Inside the computer? But—who?"

"They're kids. Irritating goddamned kids, or small people made up to look like kids. They know enough to hide when other people come around but I'm gonna kill one of the little fuckers one of these nights and we'll see who's crazy then, won't we?"

You can laugh or you can cry. Or you can sit speechless, which is what I did.

"They're filming everything," he said.

I was overcome as I squatted there, sweating like an animal, my face on fire, pushing thumb and forefinger into my eyes as if I could stanch the tears like blood-flow.

"Hey." He frowned. "Don't worry about 'em, Sam. They're punks. Every last one of 'em. I'll tell you," he slurred lower, his voice confidential now. "Sometimes they wear these skimpy dresses—and not the girls either." And without warning I began to laugh. Cross dressing little people in the heating vents! I was thinking of telling Jill about this, and shit, Grandpa Art—the real Grandpa Art—would have doubled over laughing about it if he was here, so what the hell.

"It *is* funny, isn't it? It's funny as shit!" he said, his face breaking open in a smile.

"Sometimes all you can do is laugh, right?" I said, blinking the tears away.

Grandpa Art was nodding, looking smug. "Long as those fuckers leave me be, I'm happy."

But the point is that I went back to Blackmer twice that week, just doing my penance, putting in my time with the old people. And I went again the next Sunday and stayed until after dark, and as I was leaving town, it happened.

I'd been trapped longer than I intended. The sunlight was gone as I waded out of town and I closed my cell and turned almost randomly into the Baron Square shopping center. Jill had called me and ordered a frozen pizza and a pre-mixed salad. I didn't think too much about reopening wounds, Baron Square just happened to be on the way back to the freeway. Rolling into the lot, I found that all my other memories of this little sprawl of real estate had become obscured and dreamlike, and the shopping center existed for me as the place Tommy and I had sat and waited to follow and kill what turned out to be two men.

Vanguard's big windows were lit up and cut out of the gathering darkness, and Rancho Bonita seemed to be doing decent business for a Sunday night. I craned my head and gaped at the buildings as I passed, but I was going over to the grocery store so I finally turned away. And then there was a buzz in my skull; strange pressure in my temples. I blinked and frowned. For a long moment I didn't even recognize the source of the horror I felt or entirely understand why my feet were lowering down on the clutch and brake pedals.

Headlights pressed up behind me as I stopped, but I ignored them. I looked slowly over. A little red Japanese go-cart was pulled up to the run-in-and-grab-something spot, right in front of Vanguard's doors—facing me so I could see its gray-primered fender.

There was a gentle horn tap from the car behind me and I took my foot off the brake and then the clutch, began rolling again and made the first right into a row of parking spaces.

I killed the engine, sat there in my darkened car and stared. And then I started moving, yanking the door handle, rising out of the car. I was preparing to sprint across the black pavement to Vanguard when I thought, *What in the fuck are you doing, Sam?*

What would I do when I saw him, saw his face, and imagined him in that apartment with Jill? I was getting sick with rage just seeing his goddamned car. I had taken the gun apart after...Rich. And then I had wiped down the pieces, lost them all in different places. The brass knuckles were in the bottom drawer of my dresser. Inside a fucking sock. So *what?* Would I try to kill him with my bare hands, draw witnesses, get arrested, tie it in with Jill's rape and Rich Channing lying dead down by the levee?

I settled back into my car, closed the door and waited. And there he was exiting the store, glancing left and right like he was guilty of something.

From a hundred or so yards Johnny the rapist was nothing special. His skin didn't even look especially dark from here. He was just the garden-variety Mexican-American stoner that lives in every crack and shadow in this town. He wasn't too tall but I could see he had a gym membership. His shoulders and chest were like football padding under his blue T-shirt. But he also had the gut and waist of the shameless connoisseur of the modern American diet. Except for a Marine-type haircut and a small mustache, that was all I could say about him as he dropped into his car, pulled the door shut, and the headlights came on like eyes opening wide.

I twisted the key in the ignition and shoved the Fairlane into first and pulled through an empty space, crawling toward the go-cart as it began to move. I would find out where Johnny lived. That was all, that was all…

Jesus, he wasn't going home. He parked in the far corner of a dark public lot beside a small crumbling park with weeds splitting the pavement and graffiti on every possible surface. There were basketball courts featuring backboards with the chunks broken out of them and hoops without nets. There was a patch of lawn that might barely accommodate a touch football game and, off to the side, there was an entrance to a bike trail.

The trail wound down through the swamps at the edge of town, found its way to the Conejo River and then gave exercise enthusiasts a ten-foot-wide asphalt strip to labor up and down from here to Del Mar. I rolled by on the street and slid the Fairlane up to the curb. I got out, taut and nervous, eased the door closed and laid my weight against it until it clicked.

I had a view of him through chain-link and shrubbery but he might have been alone in the universe for all he bothered to look around. He was little more than a silhouette. A living shadow amid dead ones. I watched him throw a cigarette away and immediately light another one, and I thought of him smoking all those cigarettes he got for free from Rich and the hatred flared inside me.

The town was settling quickly, everyone inside their caverns, windows glowing yellow, eating dinner, flipping channels, going to bed early. Blackmer had to work tomorrow and Johnny had the outdoors to himself. He dragged on his cigarette a moment, enjoying it, and began walking.

To the bike trail.

And it came to me as if nothing else in the world could happen. As if I'd been planning this for years. I found myself instantly behind my car, the key in the slot, the trunk clinking its release and sighing open. I looked around. A dead street. The sky a serene purple blanket. Every soul retreated into a home or apartment. I looked back down and I could make it out.

Jill and I lived in a one-bedroom apartment, so I used my trunk to store some things. There was a battered red metal toolbox loaded with my old greasy socket set, end wrenches, pliers and so forth. And beside it was my construction belt. With my 24-ounce framing hammer. I had come across the tool at a yard sale and picked it up for four dollars shortly after my wage had been raised at the construction job. I was proud of it because it seemed a sort of status symbol. Something a professional carpenter might own. It had a yellow fiberglass handle and a rubberized grip, and I had gotten so I could set sixteen-penny nails and sink them with two good whams from it. Now I snatched it up and reached for the trunk lid. But before I closed the trunk I thought again, pushed the tool belt aside and got my leather work gloves from beneath it.

I moved briskly through the shadows, thinking hard about Jill and that night, feeling the inevitability of what was about to happen, feeling myself lusting for it.

And, hell, it was easy. Or at least part of it was. There are foot trails that wind off the main bike path, and at the end of the foot trails are benches, situated in clearings where some delusional city planner imagined people sitting in silent peace, communing with nature, reading fucking Dickens maybe. And of course the bushes around the benches are always crowded with empty pint bottles, disease-ridden hypodermic needles, used rubbers and so much random garbage it looks as if someone has upended a public trash bin.

I saw Johnny's silhouette turn suddenly down one of these trails. The silhouette was impressive the way any weightlifter's is—packed with muscle through the shoulders, with a bull neck supporting a small-looking head like a cantaloupe on top of a Roman column. I wouldn't want to grapple with the motherfucker, but I didn't intend to. I followed him, stepping lightly, wearing my gloves, feeling the weight and force of my hammer.

A moment later my eyes had adjusted to the new level of darkness in this leafy nook, and I could see that he'd already sat down. There, in shades of blue and black, were those hulking shoulders, that bull neck and that black melon head rising up over the back of the bench.

I rushed up, hearing my breath suck in the darkness, and I felt the jolt of the hammerhead against his skull. It struck somewhere over the right ear and the hammer bounced off, but not all that much. The skull had given way, at least partially. He immediately sagged as if falling asleep, and I flipped the hammer around and hacked the claw into the neck, up under the jaw where I guessed the fabled jugular veins are—guaranteeing he would bleed out—I figured.

I paused. He had now slumped over until he was about to spill off the bench. The black blood was indeed surging forth, and I touched his head with my gloved fingers to steady him and raised my arm for another hack—

"What the fuck?" came the voice from behind me.

I looked over my shoulder, hammer still raised high like I was some player in a comedy sketch. I could see the guy's dirty blond hair. His narrow, almost petite frame.

"Dude, who are you? What the fuck are you doing?"

I lowered the hammer and turned to face him, and it was almost a bad joke.

My eyes were fully adjusted now, light was angling

over from somewhere, and I recognized him from high school, although I couldn't remember his name. A white-trash heavy metal kid, a year or two behind me. It was in my head so suddenly and completely that I almost wanted to exclaim it and laugh, to celebrate the recognition. In a heartbeat I saw him as he'd been fifteen years ago, a ridiculously cocky, strutting, underweight little shit with a cigarette in his mouth, the bill of his cap flipped inside-out to display the "M.O.D." written across its green underside in magic marker.

"I know you," he said. Then, "Is that a hammer? Hey, man, what the fuck are you up to, guy?" And he changed, hunkered down and was pointing something at me. It was a knife, of course. "You better get your ass out of here, guy," he said, seeming almost as if he was about to laugh. Still a cocky little shit.

I looked at him and was at a complete loss. A breeze made a sound like TV static in the leaves around us. And then, behind me I heard the sliding…a beat of pregnant silence, and then the slightly wet *fwwwump* of Johnny hitting the ground.

The heavy metal kid's eyes bugged. He pointed with his knife. "Is that…?" he said, then "—with a fuckin' *hammer?* You hit—" And he was backing up, backing up, and I finally rushed him.

I don't know what to tell you about it. I had no choice because he recognized me. He couldn't get close enough with his knife, and I kicked at him and took Viking swings with my hammer until I knocked him down as he tried to turn and run. Then I was on top of him, and I did it. I hit his neck, and when he stopped moving I hit it again and again, crushing it between the hammerhead and the crumbling asphalt walkway until I was sure the passages for air and blood had been demolished and he'd never move again.

Then I rose, huffing. Held my breath, listened to the town, and found it totally indifferent to what had happened here.

I went over to Johnny, who was a black bulk piled in front of the bench. The ground around his head was dark and glisteny, as if a five-gallon bucket of used motor oil had been dumped there. But I leapt over and did my work on his neck. Three horrid blows, with the claw this time, and if he survived it would be a miracle and he'd spend the rest of his life wishing he hadn't. He had no idea who I was anyway.

I began to walk away, then stopped over the heavy metal kid, bent and cleaned the hammerhead as best I could on his pants. If you're wondering what he was doing there, well, the brutal double murder was on the front page of the Blackmer *Sentinel* the next day. He had a roll of cash and four baggies of pot in his pockets. He was there to make the pettiest sort of drug transaction. I read his name, Dean Merriman, and immediately flashed on everyone back in Blackmer High calling him Dino. Since he hadn't been robbed, and due to the medieval nature of the crime, the article in the paper said police were looking into groups or individuals with extremist views in the area. People who might be outraged at the illicit activity that tended to take place in the dark corners of town.

But there, in the murky darkness with my bloody hammer, next to the bike path, I started to move again, remembered seeing something and went back one more time. Beside Johnny, I fished one of the half-dozen thin plastic grocery bags from the branches of the shrubbery and put the hammer and gloves inside it.

I finally walked back, crossed through the parking lot and glanced at the little go-cart. And only then did it hit me. I had never *seen* Johnny the rapist before tonight. *Jesus fucking Christ*—what information was I working off of? What if this was some other jackass in some other little Japanese go-cart with a gray-primered fender? What if I had just done this demonic thing, and had obliterated the life of *the wrong man?!?*

I stopped in the parking lot. The bodies still warm and oozing, just a few hundred yards away, the murder weapon and blood-spattered gloves in the bag hanging at my side. I stood there for anyone to see, and I walked directly up to that car. I walked around and squatted behind its rear bumper where I couldn't be seen by any passers-by. I set the grocery bag down and fished out my wallet. Was the paper still in there? I had no memory of removing it or cleaning out my wallet at any point these last several months. I shoved my index finger under the library card, behind the driver's license, beneath a few business cards—and I felt the folded piece of paper bag.

My wallet on the ground between my feet, tilting the paper toward the light, I read the license plat number I had scribbled down and...*Jesus-fuck*...

It matched.

I balled my jacket up and shoved it on the floor of my car, next to the grocery bag. Racking my brain, I remembered a gas station just a few blocks away with an outside restroom that you had to put quarters in to enter, and I drove there. No attendant to deal with, you just pulled up and paid. I had an ashtray full of change.

It was well worth the price of admission. I found blood on my cheeks and forehead and washed it off, then combed water through my hair with my fingers in case there was blood there too. My pants were newish Levis, still a deep blue, and I scrubbed the front with a wet paper hand towel. I could hardly see the spots afterward. I splashed water in my armpits and put some liquid soap up there to mask the smell. My shoes were, thankfully, old, and they were so weathered and broken down I myself couldn't tell if there was anything on them. I flipped my legs up and caught my toes one at a time and looked down, and the smooth yellow soles were clean. I hadn't stepped in—or tracked—any blood.

I took the wet paper towels with me when I left. Stuck them in the grocery bag with the hammer and gloves, and then drove back to get the frozen pizza. It had all been only a half-hour of my life. I checked as I drove and my cell hadn't rung, so I called Jill, told her I was just slightly behind schedule because I had run into some guy

I used to know and got to bullshitting, but I was getting her pizza now and would be right home. That was the danger, I said, of me coming back to Blackmer. Always running into people I know.

EPILOGUE

Maybe you've been to a funeral like this. It's early afternoon on a gray winter day. You're standing on a green hillside spotted with headstones and plaques, planted with a decade or two's worth of the deceased. You're shaved and groomed and dressed up so you feel embalmed yourself, and it's so fucking windy that you keep squinting and turning your face away, squeezing tight against the girl next to you, thinking the goddamned priest must have ordered the weather up special just for dramatic effect. Your newborn daughter keeps crying over the priest's recital, reminding everyone there of the cycle of life and death, hinting in a vague way at some redeeming, beauteous, poetic arc to everything, but you know she just needs to be changed again.

And yet you see your girlfriend, surreally attractive in

the formal dress, holding the child, bouncing and shushing her, and you can't feel too dismal—about anything.

It's more of a family reunion, really. The tears have come and gone and now you're in the company of the aunts and girl cousins and other women you're somehow related to but never see, and the uncles and male cousins who came to be pallbearers with you. Your jailbird cousin, Tommy, who ought to pay his respects if anyone ought to, is conspicuously absent. But you would have expected nothing else from Tommy.

In truth, it's a relief when someone dies like this, after running their course. Grandma Anne can go live with your Aunt Laura and Uncle Sonny now; Laura and Sonny have three daughters and you can tell the old woman's looking forward to being among them. Hers and Grandpa Art's house in Blackmer is going up for sale and money won't be an issue, so things seem to be working out. But later you'll all be in that house one last time. Surrounded by all the eerie pictures of the past and Grandpa Art's smell and presence, and you'll all take shots from his fifth of Jack Daniel's he kept up in the cupboard over the oven, someone'll go pick up a twelve pack or two, a couple of the guys will no doubt go out back and smoke a bowl, and you'll all sit around and catch up and laugh until midnight. There's no shame in admitting that you're looking forward to it.

Because if you've been to a funeral like this you'll understand that people die and that's that. Sometimes they get to die with dignity, but mostly they don't. You might worry that you could have been nicer, or could have done different, but you don't worry for long. Because what you finally understand is the dead don't give a shit. They're somewhere else, or maybe they're nowhere, but they're sure as hell not here anymore. And then maybe you realize that it's the same with the past and all your mistakes. They're dead and buried and you're still alive. Make the most of it.

www.ingramcontent.com/pod-product-compliance
Lightning Source LLC
Chambersburg PA
CBHW020618250626
47154CB00004B/1569